My R

My Renaissance

JULIA CHAMBERS

Published by Rosa Mundi Press

A CIP catalogue record for this book is available from the British Library.

ISBN 978-0-9574943-0-5

Prepared and printed by:

York Publishing Services Ltd
64 Hallfield Road
Layerthorpe
York YO31 7ZQ

Tel: 01904 431213

Website: www.yps-publishing.co.uk

Author's Note

In the early 1980s I was given a British Museum Library Reader's Pass and spent hundreds of hours in the North Library at the front desk (where I could be seen) rifling through the contents of The Private Case and The Cupboard. PC and Cup were the category markers for pornography, of which the BML had a marvellous collection, much of it bequeathed by the nutty Henry Spencer Ashbee at the turn of the last century. As a feminist who adored beautiful men and sex, I had been most disconcerted by the pronouncements of several feminist academics, most compromising perhaps being Robin Morgan's assertion that "Pornography is the theory – rape the practice". I was not adverse to a bit of salacious reading matter and had been dazzled by the gorgeous rhetoric of Angela Carter, who had managed to turn that ghastly toad de Sade into 'the moral pornographer,' if not a prince. In response I went in search of 'the female pornographer' – not the pseudonymous scribblers of the Black Lace series, nor even the women who wrote to order for Girodias and the very male-oriented Olympia Press, but women who wrote from the cunt by way of a mind that considered sexual parity with men to be a given.

I found a few gems, but nothing that would constitute a female tradition. Unlike Andrea Dworkin, I had no problem with accepting that *The Story of O* was written by a woman, but it just didn't do it for me, didn't fit my requirements. It too had been written specifically for the male of the species, and so stuffed with surrealist tableaux and Roman Catholic redemptive motifs it seemed more of a treatise on contemporary aesthetics than a turn on (although I'm sure the cerebral Jean Paulhan spent over every page).

Unable to find what I wanted, which was not the buggery and lashings (yes, I know it's all very anarchistic and naughty, but grow up), of so much of the material I dug up I determined to write my own – for want of a 'better' word – pornography. My sexual education in the BL has of course influenced the content and the form of these stories, hence the many familiar scenarios and favourite authors, including D H Lawrence whose daft sexual politics had Kate Millett spiting pricks, but I wonder if he might have got to the heart of the matter when Gudrun rebukes Gerald with 'Try to love me a little more, and to want me a little less'. From *O* I took the dressing up and the idea of the sex story as love letter: several of these tales were written with specific readers in mind – did I turn you on? And of course these are all love letters to Italy.

Some of the stories have already appeared in print, the majority in Jamie Maclean's archly sophisticated *Erotic Review*. The first to be published was a version of 'Mrs Corallo', in John Murray's *Panurge* – although the dog had to go. 'Word Play' and 'Street Life' appeared in the literary journal, *Ambit,* whose owner Martin Bax is a real Renaissance man: he somehow manages to combine the sacred duty of doctor with the profane pursuit of fine new writing and art. Thanks are due to the diligent and generous Christine Fears who edited and enhanced the stories – I'm sorry the Ferrari had to go but hey, a girl, even Julia, can't have everything. And *grazie mille* to Marialuisa.

Finally thank you to the friends and lovers over the years who have inspired and loved me – you know who you are.

Prologue

London

Turning fifty.

When did an aside become an issue?

When did a year acquire this significance? I never afforded it such.

He had wanted to say, "But you look so good for your age." He didn't, not quite.

And how should I look exactly? How do I look in fact?

My nipples are dark pink and visible through the bubbles. I run the fingers of my right hand under the water and over my belly – flat, quite flat. Never stretched by a child, never will be. I run my finger around the curve of my navel and brush back the bubbles to reveal the rose tattoo that follows it – for another decade, thirty or was it forty? And the motorbike of course. Both rather inevitable I suppose. I raise first my left leg then my right to admire the red toenails on my remarkably straight toes – remarkable when one considers how many miles they have travelled on the most absurdly high heels.

I take a sip of champagne from the exquisite Murano glass flute. I know I shouldn't use it in the bathroom, I know I'll break it soon, put it down on the white marble floor where I won't see it and crush it underfoot, filling my tender soles with myriad shards, and I will bleed all over the house. Nowhere to put it but the floor. My old bath had a wide ledge, perfect for putting things down. This roll top looks very well stood in the middle of the vast room but all necessary toiletries have to be suspended from the rolled edge in a wire basket. I always wanted such a bath and now I have one. There is not much left to want really. Nothing I can think of.

The antiquated machine clicks on again downstairs, my voice sounds young, childish almost and then the very adult voice of M– to wish me Happy Birthday. M– is my visiting man, we meet for sex and conversation, here in my home. He is unattached in every way, not even married, though marriage always seems to encourage an emotional detachment in matters of sex, which suits me. No, I draw the line at married men. More a matter of principle than morality: I have a begrudging respect for the state – sufficient to prevent me from entering it in good faith. My name has always been my own.

Like all the other voices today, below and on the mobile, M– wonders where I am. Surprised that I am not having my usual birthday celebration, sorry to have disturbed me if I want to be alone, hoping that I am not finding turning fifty too traumatic.

Not traumatic, no, not remotely, although there is something rather sad about the passing of another decade. But yes, I am disturbed, by the events of a day that should have held no more than the gentle, infinitely bearable sadness of every moment nearer the end than the beginning.

It was, as they say, bound to happen, and on this day, of all days, but yes, it disturbed me all the same. I met the American again. Midway down a still busy West End street – the very rich will always be very so – I had stopped to admire a gown in a favourite designer's window. A man stopped beside me and said, "It's beautiful, no?" And I knew him immediately. After a lifetime of the American media the accent was familiar to me but the effect of the voice on my memory was astounding. My blood was shaking and I could not breathe for fear I would gasp like a banked fish. He turned to look at me. I stared steadfastly into the window, half-afraid he had forgotten, wanting him to remember.

I finally found the breath to say, "I would look beautiful in such a dress."

The American was forgiven for his hasty departure three decades ago as I turned to face him and heard him stammer, "Julia, Julia? My God, I can't believe it, I've thought about you so often."

I simply smiled, wide-eyed with incredulity. I needed time, but I saw that age had not withered me, and how I exulted in that!

"No, it's true. So often, in fact every time I'm in London I come here to look in the window; it's a sort of ritual. Whenever I'm in Milan I go to that same shop, that same café – it's still there. I think I was hoping to meet you but I was always afraid that I might, you know, spoil it if I did. That's why I couldn't say goodbye. It was like the night never ended. I wondered if you would understand that, or if you'd think me a coward. Did you?"

I had no choice but the one I made – to engage. "Did I what? Think you a coward or understand?"

"Both. Either."

"I understood, honestly I did."

"Did you ever think about me?"

"For a while, afterwards."

He lowered his head; I think he was rather piqued. He wanted me to be hurt, wounded and still missing him.

"Well, I'm sorry anyway."

"There's no need, I had a wonderful time. But if you insist, apology accepted."

"How very English. Maybe how very Julia, but you look great, just great."

He paused and drew his lips in tight, waiting. Did he expect me to return the compliment? With none forthcoming he started again, "Look, I feel a little awkward here. Can we go someplace and talk? I mean, I really would like to talk."

I agreed to have coffee with him and we walked side by side, past the outré displays, the minimalist monochromes, the frankly ridiculous apparel and into the appropriately Italian café where he ordered two cappuccinos.

I looked at my American again. He had looked after himself; life and the years had obviously been kind and he had not changed so very much. A little broader perhaps, honestly lined in all the right places. Even the hair was as it should be, shot through with grey but still abundant – Oh Lucky Man – and still the man who had stroked my breasts in the tiny café, who had sucked my nipples dry and licked my cunt wet in the dark alley, who had fucked me in front of that mirror and into the dawn. And what did he see when he looked at me?

He lent in close, "I still have your panties." He was whispering but I couldn't resist a glance around to confirm that everyone else was talking to, or texting, someone in another dimension. I thought I would laugh but he continued, fast and soft.

"I found them in my jacket. You know, I wanted to fuck you the moment I laid eyes on you. I still want to fuck you, even now, right here. I've fucked you so many times in my head in my bed with other women. I can still taste you, smell you, feel you, your hot cunt and that beautiful mouth. I've pushed my tongue and my prick into that mouth in my dreams, daytime and night. Sometimes I'm sat behind my desk and I turn a page and there's this picture of a girl, maybe it's the eyes or the colour of the hair or even the dress, you remember that dress? You should have kept it you know. They sent it to me in New York. I got a few girls to try it. Don't be offended, it was always you inside. It's always you and I sit behind my desk and I'm so hard I can't bear it and I take out my prick and run my hands up and down it and it's like that time in the alley when we could have got caught, when someone could have walked by, someone could walk into my office, but I don't care – I just come, and you leave my head for a while."

And it worked, I was wet and the heat in my cunt was fiercer than the steam hissing through the foaming milk. I smiled indulgently and told him that I had a cappuccino maker of my own, a magnificent machine that hisses and steams and gurgles louder than Giuseppe's, dark green and shiny with chrome tubes and gold knobs. It seems an extravagance to stoke it up for me alone, but it is a ritual and a luxury I refuse to forgo.

He said he'd searched the world on the web for me, "You didn't tell me your full name."

"Nor me yours."

"But didn't you wonder about me? Google me perhaps?" His disappointment was tangible.

"Certainly not." And indeed I had resisted the technological temptation of the last ten years, in truth it had not seemed hard. It was not until now that I realised how I had missed him like a life I could have lived.

He asked about the life I had lived since Milan and I told him nothing. He offered so much information it seemed as if he'd lived three lifetimes in the three decades since we'd parted: three engagements; two marriages, the first nine months long and the second a robust 18 years but they'd "grown apart"; a son and a daughter somewhere in mid-America. He had built on the wealth he had obviously already inherited when we met and, it would appear, he now ran the entire world of glossy magazine publishing from behind some very ornate screens.

"But tell me, what about you? Are you married or something?"

"Something, perhaps."

"So, you're a free agent. I guess you always were. But surely something, someone, sometime must have got to you?"

I suddenly became aware again of where I was – in a very old black and white movie starring no one in particular. I looked at my watch and said I must go.

"Can we meet later? I'm in town for a few days, on business. I'm staying at The A-. I'm on my own more or less."

I said that it was, more or less, impossible and reached behind to draw my jacket from the chair back. The gesture pulled the cashmere tight across my chest and my state of arousal was evident.

"You still have beautiful breasts. I can see the nipples through your top, as clearly as I could through that silk blouse."

As I rose I cast him a smile I had made my own and held out my hand in farewell.

He grasped it tightly and smiled, "Don't go, not yet. You know I can't stand up – I'll get arrested for indecency."

I did laugh, and truthfully. He seemed disconcerted and let go of my hand. I lent to kiss his cologned cheek before turning to walk very smartly through the glass door which was being held open for me by a delightfully fresh young man.

I was still smiling as I walked to the square in front of my house where the trees were turning to amber and gold above the manicured lawn. No one used it apart from me, or so it seemed, apart from the gardener – another lovely boy who nodded shyly as he trimmed the borders, tended to the flowers and raked the early fallen leaves. I had tried talking to him but his monosyllabic responses and Eastern European accent deterred me from more than the politest of exchanges, which was rather a pity. Sometimes I took a book and wandered down to sit in the sun.

This time I sat on the bench and closed my eyes. A slight vibration was still thrumming in my blood and I was surprised at how quickly my body had responded to his words. It was not, however, the same as before, in the café in Milan. How could it be? London and the years aside, back then I had handed myself over to the experience, I had been a partner to the seduction, this time I had merely been a spectator, as I am always now the spectator. The breeze blew a few soft strands of hair across my cheek. I could almost imagine that I was back in the small park behind The Ambrosiana with the hum of distant traffic and its warm wooden bench. In Italy it would still be weather for naked arms and sundresses, but here it was too cold to sit for long.

I went inside to stoke up the coffee machine and retrieve the box of my memories. I determined to go back before I went forward into my 'maturity'. I wanted to meet her again, that free agent, to ask her if she was indeed the free spirit who had always eluded their grasp, or was she just afraid? But first I would take a bath.

Milano, 1981

Mrs Corallo

Four floors above the elegant shoppers on Via Monte Napoleone was my four o'clock lesson, and my first student, Mrs Corallo. The penthouse suite was reached via a mirrored lift which swished breathlessly upward and whose golden doors slid open into a domed vestibule of honey-coloured marble. There was one door opposite the lift and that too was of a dull gold metal. There was no handle on it, no lock and no bell, not any that I could discern anyway. I raised a fist to knock but then noticed a small gold box on the wall to the left of the door. When I raised the lid I found a row of numbered squares, one of which read *"prema"*, which I did. Simultaneously a light grew bright above me; no doubt I was on camera somewhere but the lens was well concealed. The door moved silently inward to reveal the most unlikely and unexpected keeper of such a fortress – a round woman with a heap of dark hair knotted on her huge head who smiled broadly and bade me enter.

Concetta was Mrs Corallo's maid and had a heart as big as her arse. She had a bosom like a shelf on which she would balance gilt trays of freshly-squeezed orange juice or homemade lemonade in tall misty glasses clinking with ice. In her large hard hands she brought plates of biscuits, dusty with icing sugar, and airy cakes, weighted down with real vanilla custard. She was a maid in heaven, but although Mrs Corallo lived so near to the clouds her home had an air of lubricity more appropriate to a bordello.

That first day I followed Concetta's generous behind through the extraordinary apartment in a state of enchantment, like an astonished gawping fish. The front door opened immediately into a great round lounge, lit by a glass dome which rendered the room an aquarium, an effect further enhanced by the huge fleshy plants that thrust glossy leaves and curly fronds upward to the light. Shiny cushions of turquoise and crimson and purple and blue were scattered across the curved white nubuck sofa like tropical jewels, and my feet sank into the plush white carpet, as soft and deep as desert sand.

There were several archways leading off this room, but I only ever went through one. This was the entrance to a long corridor whose lemon walls were strung with beads, small citrine beads that formed a curtain down either side of the tunnel, hanging from a silver rail concealing the source of the soft uplighting. Overhead the curved lemon ceiling was refreshingly clear. It was in this cool corridor that I would oxygenate my senses before succumbing to the opium den of Mrs Corallo's bedroom.

One entered through an invisible but palpable wall of tuberose and patchouli; indeed, her perfume was so heavy it remained stagnant in the room. It bludgeoned all other senses into submission, until even Concetta's cakes tasted of flowers. Once in an effort to make conversation that was not about the vagaries of English grammar I queried the origin of this olfactory sin. She leaned back in her chair, narrowed her large dark eyes and smiled – the effect was intended to be enigmatic: "*Ma cara mia, questo e il mio segreto.*"

And she guarded it well.

A more inappropriate setting for the begetting of anything other than carnal knowledge I could never have imagined, but Mrs C insisted on taking her lessons in the boudoir.

The room was surprisingly small, or maybe it was just the clutter that made it appear so. These walls too were well hung, but here red ribbons fell from cornice to floor and to every ribbon was tied every piece of bric-à-brac imaginable, and some that weren't. Beads of every kind, colour, shape and size, paper *putti*, tiny concertinas of fans, miniature carnival masks, silk and lace and paper flowers. These covered three walls. The fourth was all of glass and opened onto a balcony festooned with foliage. On either side of the glass were draped gold curtains, caught up with red cords. There was in fact very little furniture in the room; a large bed, a small white wood table with suitably ornate legs and a white chair with a red velvet seat that looked as if it had been carved by Capodimonte.

One chair, two sittees. I was ordered onto the bed and Mrs C sat on the chair opposite, the table between us. Whether this was power play or some fantasy setting I never ascertained. It was however, extremely uncomfortable. First, I was always seated on the side of the bed that faced the balcony so the glorious afternoon sun was invariably full in my face. This meant that I often left the boudoir with streaks of mascara on my cheeks where the brightness made my eyes water. Secondly, the bed was covered with the same heavy cloth as the curtains, a shiny gold lamé. Although the season was officially Spring I was determined to enjoy the continental climate and was already in Summer mode, light, bright strappy dresses with little bolero jackets in silky fabrics that were impossible to place on the lamé. I would push the heels of my hands hard against the mattress in an attempt to impede the inevitable progression of posterior to bed's edge and when I needed my hands to turn pages, gesticulate, or eat and drink, I perched birdlike on the balls of my feet, the rest of my body only glancing off the gold.

My attention to Mrs C was therefore minimal, distracted as I was by the light, the lamé and the dog. He was the major distraction, lolling against the wall opposite the end of the bed. I was always aware of the massive Alsatian that shared Mrs C's boudoir. He lay still for the most part and Mrs C assured me that he was absolutely harmless, and far too lazy to move let alone leap on me. In fact he spent almost every lesson masturbating. I had never seen a dog's prick before and when I first noticed from the corner of my watering eye the dog licking at its belly I thought that, like a cat, it was cleaning itself. When Mrs C realised the direction of my attention she laughed. She had a laugh that rang high and sweet like a child's and which always surprised me; I felt a throaty chuckle would have been more in keeping with her demeanour and her age, all of thirty six.

"*Guarda pure, che ceppo di cazzo!*"

I did as she bade me: I looked and saw the monstrous appendage and was instantly petrified.

"*Molto grande no? Gli uomini non hanno una cosa cosi, non possono dare cosi tanto gioia alle donne come Kurt.*"

She looked at me wholly unabashed, willing me to meet her eyes, willing some reaction from me other than acute embarrassment. While I was trying desperately to find an appropriate response the hours of teaching finally paid off: "Do you know the English word for *cazzo* Mrs C?"

Mrs C did what she always did at my discomfort, she laughed.

"*No cara, dimmi, dimmi.*"

"Prick, or if you wish to use the biological or medical term, penis. Prick however, is also a verb. Please look it up in your dictionary while I go to the washroom."

Mrs C continued to smile her knowing smile while I excused myself and hid until my flaming red cheeks had paled to the pink of the washroom walls. I could have stayed there the full hour, but the colour scheme was utterly nauseating and every minute away was a victory for Mrs C. I had very nearly lost my ground as her tutor; she had very nearly become mine and if truth be told I knew even then that her lessons would be far more interesting and useful.

Mrs C was one of my more able students, already fluent in French and German as well as her native Italian, she wished to add English to her many social skills and, apparently, to fill several afternoons with my company. Married to a wealthy scion of an old Lombardian family she was a legendary hostess and would entertain me with tales of outrageous dinner parties and weekends away.

She was obviously at ease in any environment and had taken charge of many situations, while I was deeply ignorant of so many things, but I resolved that the acquisition of sophistication should not necessitate the begetting of dogs. I walked purposefully across the corridor and back into the bedroom, took up my pencil and demanded the meaning of 'prick'. To put it in context, and with an ingenuity of which I am still proud, I told her the story of the *Sleeping Beauty*, pausing every now and then to note the new vocabulary – spinning wheel, spool, brambles, fairy and witch were all entered in her turquoise script in the red leather bound book she kept for our lessons.

The telling of the tale was a spell in itself. Perrault's analogy of sexual awakening so enthralled both of us that the coarseness of any earlier mutual fantasy was smoothed into a pleasant hour ended only by Concetta's announcement of a waiting guest, by which time the thoroughly sated dog had fallen asleep.

The sexual power Mrs C exercised over me was far greater than that attempted by any man. First, I had no defences against a woman: I had never had need either emotionally or sexually. I had never even guarded against my attraction to my own sex. Art classes taught me to view the female form as the zenith of beauty and consequently desire. Elsewhere in my convent school the only naked men we beheld were tortured, emaciated and nailed to crosses. A veritable pit of imagery for those of a sadomasochistic bent, but I was always drawn to the soft-faced Madonnas, those muted Murillos' and languid Leonardos'.

Mrs C had the wide dusky face of a Pre-Raphaelite muse, heavy-lidded eyes, a full pouting mouth always coated in red and a mane of black hair that she left free, unlike the well-coiffeured ladies in whose salons I enunciated my perfect English. She was not typically Milanese: she had the dark sensuality of a southern Italian, shapely and short. The only truly elegant thing about her was her shoes, and even they were just a little too well heeled to be *di moda*. As a hobby she owned one of the most exclusive shoe shops in Milan, in which I taught two members of her staff. I always entered it with feet of clay and wanted instantly to be barefoot and pedicured, ready to slip into the soft leather, to be strapped, clasped and buckled in one of those fetishistic dreams. Mrs C took great interest in my footwear, patronising me with appraising glances at my market goods with their counterfeit Gs and Vs, and on my birthday she gave me a pair of the softest, smoothest tan-coloured riding boots, so high they had to be mounted.

No, Mrs C was not like other Milanese woman. She ate the cakes and biscuits that Concetta brought, and was unfashionably voluptuous. Her clothes were unusually comfortable looking. They seemed to caress rather than constrain her, figure hugging and breast enhancing – she had a magnificent bosom of which she displayed a great deal. She was always interested in what I wore, telling me to turn around, feeling the fabric, feeling the fit. No doubt her interest in my clothes and the body on which they hung would have seemed suspect to one more worldly. But I was quite literally under her spell. From the moment I entered her boudoir, I was in her thrall. Any superior stance I took as her teacher was illusory. I could ask to see her homework, interrogate her as to sentence construction, tense and meaning, but she always made me feel as if she were indulging me and that we were just playing at teachers and pets. It was all very improper, and after only a month of lessons all pretence at learning was swept aside when she revealed herself to me as my sexual Svengali.

When assessing my appearance her hands sometimes lingered over my hips, which she would grasp and sway to observe the flare of the skirt. To gauge the length she would kneel before me and smooth the seams against my thighs, and tell me *"Troppo corto,"* or *"Troppo lungo,"* then suggest I bring it back next time for Concetta to fix.

But on this occasion, when she reached the hem her hand slid up and under my dress. She ran her manicured nails along the inside of my left thigh, naked and damp in the Italian heat. When she reached the top she rubbed the satin of my knickers with all five fingers, then she slipped one of them under the lace-edged elastic.

I do not know if I was faint from terror, from lack of oxygen because I had been holding my breath from the moment of her hand's ascent, or from an amazed desire. I thought I would fall but Mrs C's other hand clasped my right leg behind the knee. At the same instant her finger was inside my cunt. I was stood at the end of the bed and with the utmost tact Mrs C manoeuvred me back onto it, her finger ever deeper in me. I sat and stared in wonder at Mrs C's smiling face. I had lost my voice and would not have used it to bid her stop had I found it. The wonderful languor that was spreading throughout my body was emanating from her fingertips – those pressing into my thigh and my cunt. She removed her finger and wiped it slowly across her lipsticked lips. She rose from between my thighs and brought her face up to mine.

It all seemed to be happening so slowly. I knew her kiss before I felt it, such softness and strangeness. The intelligent horror at her act abated with the gentleness of her mouth – I did not taste myself, only the glossy pigment. So close her perfume had a narcotic effect and I was utterly entranced. Her hands rose to my face and pushed aside the long hair clinging damply to my neck, which she kissed and licked as if it were delicious. She then removed my bolero and slipped down the ribbon straps of my dress.

My breasts were young and small enough to go unbound and her hands covered their nakedness. When her caresses became almost painful, she kissed them – tiny kisses around each aureole until I was sure my nipples were spurting pleasure and then she sucked them, suckled me in her hot mouth. I felt fluid, and my cunt was flowing.

Until now I had been absolutely submissive, quite literally in her hands, but my need intervened. I pushed her away from my breast and while she knelt before me I pulled up my dress over my head so I was sat on the gold in only my black knickers. I swear Mrs C had never stopped smiling, and she continued to do so as she pulled them down. She didn't remove my shoe but raised one leg to free it of the elastic which she then left garlanded around the other.

I lay back against the usually uncomfortable coverlet – now cool and silky and skin friendly – and watched as Mrs C brought her fingers and her mouth to my cunt. I was so wet and wide that I could not tell how many fingers she had inside me or at what point they were joined by her tongue. She knew where to lick and where to suck and I came quickly. As the tension eased out of me I became fearful of the consequences. Would she now speak to me – break the silence and the spell?

She said nothing but was soon lying beside me. She wrapped her arms around me like a cape. The combination of her skin and the fabric of her dress against me was so erotic I thought I would debauch myself with obscene words and requests but Mrs C took my hand and placed it on her breast. I could feel the nipple through the fabric and with a calm curiosity sought to expose her beauty by unbuttoning the soft cotton shift she was wearing. The little gold buttons ran its whole length; my fingers did not tremble as I undid every one.

I was not surprised to find underneath a veritable confection of lingerie, the brassiere was of the palest, finest pink lace through which the dark aureoles showed like the hearts of roses. The fabric obviously served no structural purpose, nor did it need to – her bosom was pneumatic. I lifted the filigree straps from her shoulders and drew the lace down under her breasts, which had the effect of increasing their amplitude. I had never felt such skin before, so rich and full. The nipples rose between my curious fingers and I bent my head to kiss them.

I had sometimes looked down on my own breasts and wanted to put them in my mouth but I could not have imagined the actual sensation. When caressing myself I was always confused by the double experience of touching and being touched. Slipping my fingers in my cunt, the delight at its silkiness was lessened by the intellectual gap between giving and receiving the pleasure. Now the gap was closed, the circle was complete: I could revel wholly in the feel of a woman's body, knowing that in following my own needs I was fulfilling hers. In her body I saw the mirror of my own desire – I saw myself beneath the body of the man who had loved me and those that were yet to take their pleasure in me. Mrs C's body was a fuller version of my own. I could not feel the bones beneath her skin, as she could do mine, but we both had small waists which slipped into generous hips. I had always admired the curve and the slope from hip to knee and now I could run my hands over their beauty. I felt like Pygmalion fashioning his Galatea, or was it Narcissus falling in love with his own image?

It was Mrs C's turn to disentangle herself from my embrace and she did so to remove the undone dress which she shrugged to the floor. She then bent her arms behind her back and I saw the loveliness of a gesture that must have delighted so many men as she deftly unhooked the bra, drew the straps down her arms and flung it laughing onto the white chair. Her knickers were of the same pink lace and just as elegantly removed. For a few moments she stood naked before me, a vision of Venus with a froth of lace at her feet, then she lay down upon the bed and pulled me on top of her.

Our breasts crushed into one and I felt the burr of her pubic hair against mine. She drew my face to hers to kiss then smoothed her hands down my back and ran her fingers between my buttocks. All the while she had been moving gently beneath me, pushing against my pubis. Now she dug her fingers hard into my arse, so hard it almost hurt but the softness of her labia was glorious and she came with a shudder and a sigh that echoed in my head.

I lay back upon the bed and became aware of a shape in the doorway – it was Concetta and she too was smiling at me.

"Ma carissima Giulia, dovresti mangiare ancora torte fatte da me."

Concetta was from the South and did not believe in thinness, fashionable or otherwise, and was concerned at my recent loss of weight. The dog had not moved – a seasoned voyeur he had observed us from his vantage point opposite.

I should have been ashamed but I was delighted. I wanted to laugh, so I did. Mrs C raised herself up on her elbow and looked down on me.

"You are happy now teacher, so your student is happy too." She turned to Concetta. "È tutto pronto?"

Concetta nodded and Mrs C stood, taking my hand to pull me from the bed, said, "Enough lessons, now let us bathe and dress."

Still laughing and naked we followed Concetta's well-covered buttocks further down the lemon corridor and into a room I had never entered before. I had always used the absurdly baroque washroom opposite Mrs C's bedroom, so was amazed to find myself in a cool white space. The fading day was falling through a skylight into a huge white tub, raised on golden claws upon a black marble platform in the middle of the white marbled floor. There were no mirrors and no sinks. In the corners of the room were the same fleshy green fronds that filled the domed lounge and along the walls were marble benches on golden clawed legs, some piled high with thick black towels, others covered in exquisite glass bottles in brilliant colours, no doubt full of the heady perfumes and oils that filled the air and floated in the blue water.

"This is my husband's bathroom. Do get in, the water will be just right."

I walked to the altar of our ablutions, and looked down on the shrine of my body at which Mrs C had so recently worshipped. I don't know if it was the light overhead, the voice bidding me enter the water, the fragrant steam rising like incense or the almost holy nature of the experience but I was suddenly in another place before another bath, between another two women.

I remembered a Summer in Lourdes and the time I went to bathe in the blessed waters, more out of curiosity than faith, of which I had very little even then. A stout old woman had told me to remove all but my bra, and put on a blue cotton cape. I had asked for a towel but was assured I would not need one – the water was so cold it would evaporate off my skin. Then I was led to a pair of blue and white striped curtains which miraculously parted, revealing a thin nun and a busty young girl, both with their sleeves rolled up, smiling in front of a concrete horse trough. One of them whisked off the cape, the other my bra and a damp pink camisole was slapped over my offending breasts. They led me down the steps into the icy water. I had to kiss a plastic statue of the Virgin at the far end of the trough while they chanted a few Hail Marys.

"We are going to lower you into the water, relax, you'll be safe."

I remember a strange dullness in the air, my body was numb. I did not feel the water on my skin but was aware of it tightening. For several hours after the bath it was as if my skin had shrunk.

I looked down on my now adult form, seeming to bloom with the moisture in the air. I looked down on my adored breasts with the blue veins marbling the white and the dark pink aureoles. I thought of the small-breasted virgin, unknowing and untried, not quite believing but so hopeful, in the icy bath in Lourdes and felt the tears brimming at the edges of my eyes. Was it sadness or nostalgia or relief at her passing? The old shames rose like a shroud from my past to cover my present glory. I drew my arm across my breast and my hand over my pudenda.

"You are my Venus, *cara*. Botticelli imagined you – I have *la realtà* here with me."

She was before me now and cupped my face in her hands. "Look at me *cara*, why are you sad? You were so happy. You must not be sad. Smile for me, *mia bella Venere.*"

She raised my chin on her fingertips, as delicately as if my head had been a butterfly balancing there. I looked into her lovely dark eyes and saw myself reflected, a goddess of her desire, and the pale young thing I was formed a tear on my cheek, which Mrs C kissed away.

"*Vieni, cara.*"

She stepped into the bath and turned to take my hand to help me in. The water on my skin was bliss. We sat at either end of the vast tub and a magician Concetta produced two crystal stems bubbling with champagne from out of the moist air. I poured the stinging golden liquid down my parched throat, any remnant of regret dispersing with the bubbles, and felt as rich and lovely as a fairytale princess. I had wandered not into a bathroom but another world.

Mrs C raised the champagne bottle from the floor beside the bath and moved towards me with a wicked smile: "I will wash my Julia, Concetta, leave us alone."

Concetta took the empty champagne glass from my hand, turned on her low shabby heels and walked out of the room. Mrs C slid towards me, the soapy water lapping around her buoyant breasts. She lifted the bottle to my lips and ran the champagne into my mouth. I swallowed but the champagne was coursing down my chin. Mrs C licked it off then poured what remained in the bottle over my breasts. My skin was so shocked at the coldness I did not immediately sense Mrs C's tongue slipping around and over my nipples. She raised her head to kiss me as she lowered the bottle onto the floor, but her lips still tasted of champagne. She kissed me so long and so hard I drew back for breath. Mrs C laughed and told me to stand, which I did, the water around my knees and running down my body.

She remained kneeling in the tub looking up at me and parted her lips, pushing the tip of her tongue between her smile and applying its coolness to the bud of my clitoris, now visible in the midst of my wet pubic hair. As she licked she slid her hands up my thighs, then into me, up to my cervix and I came, the walls of my vagina closing around her long fingers. I felt them leave my cunt and the cold air on my clitoris as Mrs C lay back in the tub, spreading her legs.

I knelt down in the water between her knees and ran my hands up and down her soapy thighs while she pleasured herself. Her head was thrown back over the white curve of the bath edge and her breasts rose and fell impossibly full in time to the rhythm of her fingers. Her nipples were so perfectly round I wanted to bite them off and roll them in my mouth. As I leant forward to suck them Mrs C came and her whole body shuddered and the breath caught in her throat. Lost in herself, I watched her and realised I wanted so much to be her, under her skin, inside her body. I wished more than anything to have a hard penis to put in her softness, to spurt inside her like champagne, to wrap my arms around her as she wrapped her legs around me.

She raised her head and opened her eyes: "*Basta, cara.* Enough love making for today."

Mrs C called for Concetta, who brought towels from the benches to wrap around us. She helped us both from the bath, then devoted herself to me while Mrs C pulled on a huge black towelling robe. At some point Mrs C must have left the room but I did not notice, I was too immersed in Concetta's attentions to my toilette. She rubbed me briskly with the fluffy towel, drying every part of my body, even between my toes. She then took a pot of cream from the nearest bench and smoothed the white lotion all over me. I recognised the heady aroma of Mrs C's scent and for once succumbed to its intoxication. I was too stunned by the recent welcome assault on my senses to fight off another. The perfume hung around me for days and permeated every piece of clothing I wore. She dusted me with silky powder and sat back upon her heels to admire her handiwork, smiling proudly as if she had just dressed me for my first communion, despite the abandonment of my clothes in a far room. As if on cue, Mrs C appeared in the arched doorway, her arms full of bright colours.

"Here Julia, now I will dress you as you should be dressed. I chose these for you after our first lesson. I know now how you feel, but I always knew how you should look, and it isn't like me, though you think you want to. No, you will be Julia, my beloved, our beloved."

She threw the confusion of colours and textures on a bench and from it pulled first a haze of lingerie in pale green. The near-transparent bra served only to accentuate my breasts and when she pulled an apricot camisole over my head my nipples could clearly be seen pointing through the silk. Concetta knelt again at my feet and lifted first one foot then the other into her lap to slip on the sheerest ivory stockings, which needed no suspenders to hold them up, a sliver of elastic and lace circled each thigh and further heightened my divided sense of clothing and nakedness. I had to step into a peppermint green skirt, so short it barely covered the lace tops of the stockings, and a pair of ivory-coloured shoes with low gold heels.

Mrs C then handed Concetta a tailored jacket with narrow lapels. It was the same colour as the skirt, but lined in the apricot of the camisole. As Concetta slid it up my arms and onto my shoulders I felt as if I were donning the soft water of the bath from which I had just risen. Concetta stood back smiling and Mrs C came towards me with her hands full of pearls. She clasped a pair of baroque drops on my earlobes and a long rope of milky globes around my neck.

"We are almost done, come."

She took my hand and led me back along the corridor, Concetta waddling behind, and into her familiar washroom. She sat me down upon the velvet-covered stool and took a silver-backed brush from the vanity unit. She stroked it through my damp and tangled hair, which she swept up into a pleat and fastened with a myriad of hairpins that Concetta passed to her over my head. She brushed apricot powder along my cheekbones and painted my mouth with coral. I gathered she had finished with me when she blotted my lips with her own – as her tongue slipped between them I grew immediately wet and my heart began to race. She gently rebuffed my proffered embrace. "I do not want to spoil our handiwork. Look how beautiful you are."

I turned to the mirror at my side and saw that I was indeed beautiful. The fragile colours of my clothes contrasted strongly with the honeyed richness of my skin, which felt as if it were straining at the fabric in its eagerness to be once again naked under Mrs C's admiring eyes. I was as elegant and sexually self-assured as any Milanese and to the reflection of my lover I said, "It is you who have made me beautiful."

She smiled with her whole radiant face.,

"And I have made you happy, no more sad Julia. But now you must go, my husband will be here soon."

I must have experienced a second's jealousy and several moments' curiosity as I thought of the man who shared Mrs C's bed and body, her past and her future. He filled my thoughts as I sped down in the lift and his imagined face was so strongly impressed upon my mind's eye that the reality did not immediately register as the lift doors swished open and there he was before me.

"*Buonasera signorina.*"

I blushed furiously and fled silently past him into the darkening evening over his shoulder. It must have been him – that lift only went to the penthouse. I hurried out into Via Monte Napoleone and was half-amazed to find it still there. Nothing changed, apart from the light, apart from me.

Coffee, Brioche and Honeycaps

I had arrived in the sharp bright spring of 1981 at Malpensa, a shabby airport on the industrial outskirts of Milan, brimful of excitement and trepidation and wholly unprepared. I had come to Italy to escape the winter and because I could think of nothing better to do.

I was following in the footsteps of a friend who had worked for a rather dodgy language school that required no more skills of its teachers than a degree in any subject, from any college anywhere. Having lost my faith in the bearded gods of my Northern university, the pursuit of a higher education seemed as appealing as entering a nunnery (though the thought had crossed the vacant lot of my adolescent mind). Moreover, I had found no substantial employment so I decided on opting out of the system for a while to consider my future. This was then a very fashionable thing for the over-educated and under-developed children of indulgent parents to do. I told mine I needed to broaden my horizons and improve my Italian, and although aware that I was not the worldliest of individuals nor the most practical, they concluded that their flowerchild would probably bloom in the sunshine of Italy. To the Italians I must have appeared as a straggly weed in their ornate but immaculate garden.

Being a reasonably good looking girl, naturally blonde, blue eyes, 5'7", albeit a few pounds over the fashionable weight, I was not unused to the occasional admiring glance. This however, was different. From the moment I strode through customs, excited at my arrival yet fearful of being found in possession of absolutely nothing, I was aware of the stares. I eventually had to concede they were not flattering. Something was wrong but what exactly was not clear until I stopped two young women and enquired as to the whereabouts of the Milan-bound coach. They said nothing but their eyes darted over my body like those of startled rabbits. They were utterly transfixed by my appearance, which seemed perfectly fine to me but in retrospect and in situ was probably more than any self-respecting Milanese could take.

Hopeful of a rise in temperature I had dressed for the sunshine and was perturbed to see that many of the people milling around the concourse were jacketed and well-shod. Perhaps it was my unseasonal attire, perhaps it was the clogs or the skirt, verdant green sunray pleats shot through with sparkles of metallic rainbow-coloured thread. It could even have been the blouse, a marigold cheesecloth confection that gaped from my waist to my neck where it fastened with satin ribbons of gold. It was however, the hat – black raffia and covered in brightly coloured flowers – they could not take their eyes off it.

I was young, scared and tired enough to be shaken by my obvious sartorial blunder and felt the blood rise to my pale cheeks. I asked them again in a voice quivering with tears, and fearing the dambreak of my distress more than social opprobrium they finally unhinged their jaws and more than compensated for their rudeness by offering me a lift to Milan. They had just dropped off a friend going to England and professing to be impressed with my Italian, welcomed me into their red Alfa Romeo in the hope that some kindly Englishman would do the same for their friend when she arrived solo and lonely at Heathrow. I doubted it, but said no more than "thank you" and bundled myself, my skirt, hat and suitcase onto the bench of a back seat.

These wonderful women, Pina and Olivia, chattered all the way from Malpensa to Milan, talking so fast I had little time to answer one question before they were on to the next. The scenery through the industrial suburbs was drab and disappointing so I kept my eyes on my companions, who seemed to me the most beautiful women I had ever encountered. They were both in their late twenties, both brunette and brown-eyed with perfect bodies over which the fine fabrics of their clothing fell like a lover's caress. Pina was wearing a dark blue silk blouse, sufficiently undone to intimate a magnificent unsupported cleavage. Olivia was more formally dressed and when I admired her suit was honest enough to suggest that I buy some new clothes – after all Milan was the fashion centre of

the world. She offered to take me shopping but even, ignorant of these matters, knew that she went not so much up market as celestial.

Recuperating from the financial traumas of student-hood, I declined but decided then and there that I would get myself some style, if nothing else.

My hippyness was discarded in an instant. The other things I had brought with me, my innocence, optimism and childish things, took longer to put away, but it was a start.

These two gave me my first taste of Italy – coffee. They insisted on stopping at a bar and the bitter dark aroma enveloped me and permeated my senses forever. Even now when I smell fresh coffee I close my eyes and smile as creamily as *schiuma* on espresso. Then I simply clapped my over-ringed hands together in delight at the thought of taking the first real cappuccino of the rest of my life. The girls were indulgent of my excitement, they found it quaint and rather endearing, as did many of the sophisticates I was soon to meet, even asking the cameriere to bring me another with a thicker coating of chocolate. They also ordered warm brioche, a delicious sweet bread Italians eat for breakfast, which melted like butter in my coffee-hot mouth and filled the pleats of my skirt with crumbs. The girls drank espresso.

We exchanged addresses and they gave me their phone numbers. I could not believe my good fortune in finding friends so quickly; I was yet to learn that such gestures were typical of the Milanese and did not denote the slightest intention to actually pursue a relationship. But then, unknowing and grateful, I thanked them profusely

when they dropped me outside my new home. I had been warned the Italians kissed on both cheeks and Pina left lipstick on either side of my smile. Olivia placed her red lips on mine. I was momentarily shocked but it was over so quickly I wondered if she had just missed.

She smiled and raised an exquisitely manicured hand to my hot cheek.

"*Divertiti cara,* enjoy yourself and get some new clothes!"

Until I could find alternative accommodation it had been agreed that I stay with the other teachers. Five of these untrained tramellers of my mother tongue co-existed in total disharmony in a two-bedroomed company apartment on Via Calzecchi. There was the plucky Welshwoman Megan, who shared one of the bedrooms with 'little Sam' as he was known. A tall, thin George shared the other one with a short, round Cecily – Lee for short – and I shared the lounge with Jack and the constant rumble of goods trains that chundered past the patio doors from four in the morning until midnight.

The few quiet hours in my makeshift boudoir were filled not with blessed sleep, but with thick smoke from the joints Sam and George and Lee and Jack would suck on to anaesthetise them to the imminent audial torture of the trains and their student's voices the next day.

It was during these hours that I became friendly with Megan. I smoked not at all and she smoked only the legal kind of cigarettes; wholly disapproving of the outrageous

activities in the lounge she would sit in the kitchen talking and drinking between drags while I coughed, chronically allergic to any cigarette's smoke.

In fact Megan disapproved of so many things I sometimes wondered why I was acceptable to her. There were to be many occasions on which I shocked her rigid, but by then she was fond of me and she never faltered in her affection. The price I paid for my subsequent 'bad' behaviour was a sermon as regular and rhetorical as a Baptist minister's but much, much funnier. Megan was a stickler for convention and never broke free of her small town background, but she was as vulgar as Falstaff and did me the great service of puncturing my prudery very early on.

I grew to love her singsong accent which was so pronounced you could tell which students were hers by the way they said "vegge taa bles," "tuuthbrush" and "up yer bum" when 'cheers' would have sufficed. Raised in the valleys, English was her second language and when she spoke on the phone to her people back home there was nothing familiar in the metre, inflections or sounds she made. She did however, use a great many Anglo-Saxon words I did recognise.

I did not swear often. 'Shit' was reserved for situations of such awfulness that I could not find an appropriate decent word to express my fury. Megan and the others used 'shit', 'fuck' and 'bugger' as readily as 'please' and 'thank you', and soon I had not only added them to my rapidly expanding vocabulary but had acquired their equivalent in Italian. This was imperative after I had stunned my fifth class, a group of sales assistants at a top Milanese fashion house, by declaring that a fabulous looking woman in a skintight white dress (lycra had not as yet stretched to British bodies) had a beautiful figure. This sounded like '*figa*', which meant to Italian ears I was enthusing on her cunt.

When my students had contained their laughter we spent what remained of the hour on the naming of parts. I took an unexpected pleasure in pointing out to them that if 'figure' sounded like female genitalia in Italian, every time they insisted they couldn't do something they were using the English term. Italians are incapable of pronouncing 'can't' as anything other than 'cunt'.

They told me a few words, I told them a few, my natural tendency to embarrassment abated by the professional setting and a growing ease with a race who spoke of sex as if it were obviously the most interesting and relevant topic for any conversation. I warned them of polite society's dislike for 'cunt', which, although used by and older than Chaucer, had become a term of abuse, unlike '*figa*' which when accompanied by a certain gesture – the palm upraised with the four fingers resting on the thumb – implied that the woman was delicious enough to eat. D H Lawrence had insisted that part of a woman actually resembled the split fruit; I wasn't so sure, but "*che figa*" followed any blonde foreigner around Milan like a greeting.

My favourite students were the children. In my first weeks I was given several to teach as a way of breaking me in to the system. Their enthusiasm and joy in our lessons delighted me, I found I adored them, unlike Megan who believed all Italian minors to be spoilt brats and me to be sentimental and dangerously broody. The idea of pregnancy and childbirth was abhorrent to her; childrearing a boring and unrewarding occupation. She determined to take me to a medical student who dished out the pill to good Catholic girls like aspirin, but I protested I had little cause for contraception.

I was a virgin when I went to college, and although I had many friends of the opposite sex I gave my maidenhead to a much loved older and experienced man of several years' friendship who had appeared up North one dismal weekend in my first term laden with flowers, champagne and what he now considered a licit desire for me. He continued to fête me throughout my student years and took the necessary precautions throughout our sweet affair until I came to Milan. We had decided it best to end things there: I was too young and he told me he had fallen in love with me. I did not understand then what he meant and why it was a problem, but I missed him, and the sex.

It was Mrs C who was instrumental in maintaining my ostensible virginity. After our first sexual encounter she asked me what I used and when I blushed to tell her what I thought was obvious – that I had no need – she smiled her Mona Lisa smile and said, "*Non ancora*. Not yet."

When I arrived for our next lesson Mrs C was waiting in the lobby and hurried me into a taxi that took us to Monza, famous for its Royal Park and racing track, and the residence of Mrs C's gynaecologist. He fitted me with a little known device called the honey cap, a diaphragm impregnated with honey, a natural spermicide favoured by the Ancient Egyptians. It needed no malodorous or numbing creams and I stored it in honey when it wasn't secreted in its chic compact or in my own honeypot. I was delighted and waited for the bees to come running. I became an advocate of the fragrant dome but Megan declined a trip to Monza.

Whether by design or felicitous coincidence, Megan was unlikely to need worry about such things since her partner Sam was sterile following treatment for infantile leukaemia and her lover, a student she called Mr Balls, suffered from premature ejaculation. He, however, was as kind and generous as Sam was mean and indifferent. When Sam got drunk he was an absolute thug, his cut glass vowels slurring in obscenities, his manners those of the gutter. I think Megan stayed with him out of pity and habit. There was no love lost between them and when they returned to England they went their separate ways.

Fortunately for her, she wasn't overly keen on sex. Unfortunately for me, Lee and George were sex mad. When they weren't teaching or drinking they were smoking and fucking – the foreplay usually took place in the lounge. I found this excruciatingly embarrassing and spent my time wandering between the kitchen and the bathroom while they determined on a cut off point for exhibitionism. When I returned to the room on their departure I would find Jack glazed and supine on the sofa. I would lower the lights, slip under the blankets on my camp bed and turn my face to the wall with a timid "good night," to which Jack never responded.

It was Megan who sowed the first seed of fear in my mind that Jack may have designs on me, then Sam and Lee and George watered it with their snickers and asides. At first I did not believe them, as I was painfully convinced that Jack did not like me. Beyond sharing sleeping quarters, a situation forced on him by the coupling of the other occupants of the apartment and remedied by the occasional night away from Via Calzecchi, he seemed to avoid all conversation and contact with me. Besides, I did not desire Jack. How much of this was due to feeling he would rather sleep with a cat than me and how much my discomfort at his indulgent voyeurism I could not honestly ascertain because I was aware that I should find this man attractive. He was very tall and well-built, and when his eyes weren't bloodshot with dope, they were a rather pretty hazel. His hair was dull brown with soft floppy curls. His nose had been broken in a rugby scrum but his smile was wryly amused and sometimes I wondered how it would feel to be in his big embrace.

I was already lying on my skeletal sleeping platform when Jack ambled in. He did not put on the light but made enough noise to wake a hookah-doped pasha on pillows as he undressed and cursed at the knotted laces in his new brogues. I heard the slight lisp in his voice, amplified by the alcohol that was spilling into the dark air from his beleaguered lungs.

Finally he wrenched himself free of the clothing that fell and thudded to the floor between us. I sensed the sofa give a little as he lay upon it and all was quiet, for a while.

"So how about it?"

I said nothing.

"I know you're awake. So how about it? How about you and me and sex?"

I held my breath and feigned death.

"Never mind, it can wait."

I maintained my corpse-like state until I heard Jack's breathing blur into a gentle snore, then exhaustion carried me off. The next day I began a serious search for new quarters.

Via Zingara

Danielle was uncharacteristically shy – hardened to the overt charm of all other Milanese males I encountered I was surprised at his reticence in manner and mode of dress, both of which were rather low key. He sported jumpers and corduroy trousers with what looked suspiciously like hacking jackets when he ventured out from the innocuous atmosphere of the office where I taught him and his three female colleagues twice a week. When compelled to use it in response to my questions his voice was soft and hesitant, otherwise he never spoke. His silence may have had something to do with the garrulous women, who hardly drew breath in their enthusiastic attempts at English. They told me that Danielle was married with three young children and lived near Como in a beautiful house which compensated for the long daily journey to Milan.

I did not form particularly strong alliances with any of these students. The women removed my name from their Fendi address books when they suggested I buy a fur coat while in Milan and I told them I neither ate animals nor wore their skins. The only social conscience I ever detected in any Milanese was exercised in determining whether to remain faithful to Valentino or abscond to the bright new camps of Versace and Armani. I was thought to be extremely odd but they put this down to my English upbringing, synonymous with bad taste and eccentricity.

Danielle was to prove almost as much a major mover in my Italian life as Jack. I was desperate to move out of the dope-filled inferno of Jack's smouldering lust, so desperate that I asked every student if he or she knew of anywhere I could put my suitcase for a few months, cash in hand, promise to leave, but due to the commendably socialist laws of *ecquo canone* which protected tenants by controlling rents and outlawing eviction no one with any property ever dared to let it. There were acres of empty living space in Milan and thousands of people living in square inches.

When the women had chattered out of the office one day, Danielle hung behind.

"Miss Julia, I help you no, to find place?"

"Thank you Danielle, do you know of someone with a place to rent?"

"No someone, if you not tell any one, I have place for you."

I smiled at his syntax and his secrecy but promised never to reveal the identity of my landlord. Danielle seemed unsure, but continued: "I, my friend, he has one small place, near to Buenos Aires Road – you have it for small time."

"Danielle, I am very grateful – even for a short time. How much does your friend want for the rent?"

"Nothing, but you go when he need flat."

In Italian I ascertained that this meant no notice, not that I would have to vacate it for the odd night when his friend needed a bed in Milan. He assured me it was basic, but clean, warm and comfortable. He wrote down the address, Via Zingara, off Corso Buenos Aires, and told me I could move in the following day. His final muffled words on the matter were that he would rather I didn't mention to his colleagues that I was moving into his friend's flat, and I was touched by the kindness that had caused him to risk his reputation, even his marriage, to help me out of my predicament. I struggled to find the Italian equivalent of the soul of discretion, but he finally understood and we shook on it.

I packed that night and left my malodorous apartment in Via Calzecchi early the next morning. I deposited my suitcases at the station and took all my lessons in the best of humour – excitement at my new abode growing with every hour. Corso Buenos Aries was the High Street of Milan, full of those essential emporia that the shoppers on Monte Napoleone never entered, but to which they sent their Philippino maids. It ran from the Giardini Pubblici to the Piazza Loreto, where they strung up Mussolini and his mistress, and was always teeming with people and traffic.

Via Zingara was near the park end and remarkably quiet due to the tunnel effect of high buildings hedging a narrow street. Hardly any sound or any light entered this street but the smells hung like fog along it. There were several ristorante, a couple of café bars and a launderette, all emitting their own aromas – fresh coffee and brioche in the morning, something savoury midday and evening and the sweet smell of soap and drying linen all day and all night. At the far end of the tunnel white lights burned, bright or indistinct depending on what time I entered, forming the canopy to a 24 hour cinema. I had been living in Via Zingara for two weeks before I walked its full length searching for a chemist and discovered that it was showing *Labbie Insatsabile* and had been doing so for the last six months. I never ventured there again as the would be punters found an English blonde even more interesting than the lurid publicity shots on the walls of the cinema – Italian men have no shame when eyeing up the opposition.

That first evening I took the Metro to Corso Buenos Aires and hauled my cases up the stairs, crunching a few syringes underfoot and thumping the occasional junkie in my way. I was not as inured to their presence as they were to my knocks, although I knew that the parks and subways were the places for dealing. The drug trade was open in Milan, and so was drug taking: all the supermarkets stocked syringes. I saw many kids shooting up on the steps of the Metro and in the evenings the parks were heady with the aroma of hashish rising from circles of blissed out Italianetti who arrived on vespas and sped home on Moroccan wings. The Metro at Corso Buenos Aires was a particularly popular haunt as several of its exits led directly into the park, which was bordered by four main roads but unfenced.

A few weeks before I came to Via Zingara a baby had been murdered in the park by a junkie. He had broken its neck trying to rip off its gold crucifix, and while I was living in the area a woman had her ear lobes shredded by another desperado wanting to pawn her diamond studs. Danielle had insisted that although the apartment was safe I should not enter the park or the Metro after dark when they became the underworld of Milan.

There was still a pink glow in the sky high above the tall, old tenements of Via Zingara but the antique pulley doorbell added to a growing sense of eeriness and I was not in the least surprised when after a few moments and the sound of shuffling feet the female equivalent of Quasimodo heaved the hefty door open. She was squat and dirty and never looked up –in all the time I was there I never saw her face.

She was obviously expecting me and bade me follow her; she did not offer to help me with my luggage. The door opened into a small dark courtyard. The *portineria*'s quarters were off to the left and through an open door I saw in the flickering light from the TV a small boy sat on a table piled high with crockery and pans. He was eating from them, all of them, taking lumps of food with his hands and cramming them into his mouth. The woman must have been aware of the direction of my gaze and bellowed, "*Scendi, Paolo, bestia!*"

The child looked up – I could not make out his features as he had his back to the screen, but he must have smiled and I saw a flash of bright teeth – he was as happy as a proverbial pig in shit.

"*Bestia, bestia,*" muttered Quasimoda shuffling to a huge double door on the other side of the courtyard where she gave me three keys – one for the street door, one for this door and one for the apartment itself which was on the fifth floor, at the top. She turned and left and I turned the key into another courtyard, but this one was closed in and at its centre was a large metal cage forming a great square column that rose the height of the building. The five floors were tiered around it, each floor with a iron railed walkway all the way round and joined to the column at one point with a pier-like extension. It was quaint but precarious and I was terrified of heights. The cage contained the lift – a rather elegant wooden box with two engraved glass-fronted doors, brass handles and floor buttons. It was entered by way of a heavy spring-loaded gate which crashed back behind me as a rousing introduction to the cacophony of rumblings, shakings and squealings that accompanied me to the top floor.

There were four apartments on each floor, one door in each corner of the square. I walked all four sides, close to the wall, my heart in my mouth, my eyes straight ahead, horribly aware of the drop on the other side of the waist-high railings before I realised my flat was the closest to the lift. Perhaps the altitude had heightened all my senses but when I put my suitcases down to unlock the door I became aware of another presence, other than my fear, and knew that I was being watched. The square was well lit but the corners were in shadow. Across the gaping hole I stared brazenly and unseeing into each one until I heard a distinct click. Someone curious no doubt and well warned of my arrival – the Queen of Sheba could not have had a louder fanfare than the unoiled decibels of the lift shaft.

The apartment was tiny but well-designed, every square inch had been thought through, the epitome of purpose built – it was a lovenest. There was a small kitchen area, crystal glasses, a couple of exquisite porcelain coffee cups, nuts and crisps in the cupboard, a bottle of whiskey and cans of Coke in the fridge. There was a double bed that obviously served as a sofa as well, a fold up table, two fold up chairs and a shower room off the tiny area serving as a walk-through wardrobe.

The decor was sparse but above the bed was a mildly erotic line drawing of a naked man and woman embracing, on it a great fur coverlet edged with what looked like cats' tails. I rolled it up and put it under the bed, my nose already twitching at the long white hairs.

I was delighted with my romantic garret, but determined not to starve up there and once I had unpacked I descended to the street and the nearest ristorante. I was not uncomfortable eating on my own, and the food in such places was so good and so cheap it was the most economic way of getting a decent meal. This particular restaurant had a large TV screen high on the back wall where you could fix your eyes rather than on the surrounding faces, wondering at so much loneliness and so little etiquette as *sugo di pomodoro* splattered down chins and shirt fronts and red wine ringed the paper tablecloths. I grew to feel at home in this place and ate there several times a week, timing my visits with the daily showings of Dallas – such a novelty with the dubbed Italian voices.

I would awake every morning with the sun pouring in through the tiny window, cascading over me like warm water. I would make myself a cup of tea, the only one of the day, shower, dress and decorate myself and go down to the café opposite for a cappuccino and brioche. After the first week the proprietor, a short, round man called Giuseppe, would whisk a frothy cup onto the bar as soon as I walked in. He was very chatty and coming from Capri felt kindly towards a foreigner like himself.

The only drawback to my comfortable and convenient home was the obvious curiosity of my neighbours, with whom I had no real contact until one day my kettle blew up in a flash of blue light and I bought a new one. In those days the plug was not fitted to the appliance and although I stared hard at the sealed unit, so different from our three-pronged affairs, I could not conceive of a way of inserting the cord which had only two wires, both of them black.

I thought of the other three doors on my landing behind which lurked the natives and their prying eyes – if not friendly they would at least know how to fix my plug. The thought of starting my day without a cup of tea drove me out of my apartment and up to one of the dark wooden portals. I knocked and the almost immediate opening made me wonder if someone was stood behind it all the time, just to make sure she or he didn't miss a single one of my exits or entrances.

A slight but elegant woman in a dark blue dress and huge pearls raised her grey-haired head to meet my eyes with an undisguised look of disgust: "*Si, che cosa vuole?*"

In a suddenly stilted Italian I explained that I needed a plug fitted and would be grateful of her help. She told me it was a man's job, couldn't I find one to fix it? I was confused by her aggression. The Milanese were invariably hospitable, if shallow and insincere. But I persevered and explained my situation as a lonely teacher of English, temporarily lodging in the vacant *pied à terre* of a student. She became intensely inquisitive – where did I teach? Whom did I teach? Did I live on my own?

"*Signora*, why do you ask?" my voice faltered under the assault but indignation spurred me on. "From your constant surveillance I am sure you know more about me than I know myself."

I turned back towards my apartment, anger at her rudeness stinging my eyes.

"*Mi dispiace, ma le prego di tornare e lasciarmi spiegare.*"

Aware of a shift in power and now curious, I graciously returned to forgive her. She invited me into her gilded abode, crammed with antiques and huge oil paintings in ornate wooden frames, and told me she had thought me a prostitute, like the previous residents of my apartment.

I laughed uncomfortably, unsure of whether I was flattered or appalled at the notion, and asked again about my kettle.

"My son, Luigi, he will come later to fix it, he will know how. He will be home soon."

I declined her offer of coffee and cakes and returned to my erstwhile whore's house to await the handyman. I waited one hour then two, my anxiety growing with every shuddering of the rising lift, but he did not come. Weary with the day and the Cinzano I drank while marking, I decided that Luigi was not going to fix my kettle that night and regretted not purchasing a little saucepan to heat the water for tea in the morning. Perhaps I could use the coffee pot.

I undressed and showered, smoothed a creamy sweet lotion all over my body and face and was wondering on the whereabouts of my nightie when there was a knock at the door.

"*Signorina, sono io, Luigi*. I hope I am not too late."

I managed to emit a "one moment please" while I scrabbled for sufficient and suitable cover, but found only the shabby robe I had brought with me from home. I pulled it around me and opened the door.

And what a vision was there. Six foot of glorious young man, with a head of golden hair, emerald eyes ringed with long honey brown lashes and a strong Roman nose beneath which his lips had the sweep of archangel's wings. In silent awe I beckoned him in. I gathered he was making profuse excuses for the lateness of his visit, but his guilt-stricken mother had insisted I needed him tonight.

"I must have taken you from your bed," he said in a silky Italian accent.

I stammered something about "not at all" and hated the high notes in my usually soft voice. I forced myself to meet his eyes, but they were lowered – I thought perhaps in shyness then I realised he was looking at my naked feet with their painted toes. I quite involuntarily adopted the first position. Ribboned into ballet shoes as a child it was a stance I always affected in standing moments of uncertainty. The movement made him aware of the impolite direction of his gaze and he blushed. I blushed too and clutching my robe tight around my body began to babble on about the kettle and my needs and if he could fix it how grateful I'd be.

He picked up the plug and told me it was really very simple, but he needed a special tool he had for precisely this purpose and which he would fetch from his apartment. He left and I stood for one moment gazing into the space this beautiful man had left behind him. The air was still vibrating with his voice which resonated in my blood, thrumming through me like fingers on strings. I inhaled deeply and pulled the cord of my robe tighter around me, then knelt to look under the bed for my slippers.

I heard Luigi push the door open but persevered in my search. I was aware that my raised buttocks could be seen as a welcoming gesture, but my fast beating heart and the way Luigi had fixed on my toenails made me feel the slippers to be a necessary aid to my honour. I found them and rose to sit upon the bed. Luigi was stood before me, and smiling.

"Let me help you *signorina*. I am no Prince Charming but you are as beautiful as *La Cenerentola* at the ball."

He took the tacky gold slippers I had purchased in the market and fitted them to each foot with the same care Mrs C's staff exercised when fitting their clients' Trussardis. He then held out his hands and gently helped me from the bed. He held my hands until I could feel the heat of his fingers warming the cool tips of mine – Luigi's physique glowed with good circulation – then withdrew and walked to the table where the kettle stood tall amongst the tiny cups.

"Now let us try the plug."

It was of course fitted in minutes and much to my disappointment I realised Luigi would now have no good, or rather, Christian, reason to be in my boudoir.

"Can I offer you something? To drink that is: tea, coffee?"

My heart was pounding so hard I thought he must hear it in the seemingly endless silence that followed my clumsy importunings.

"Do you have any Amaretto?"

"Ah," I sighed, desperately disappointed.

"I see you don't, I will bring some. But please yes, I would like a coffee," and he was gone, again.

For myself a strong sedative would have been preferable, but I prepared the coffee. I would never have slept that night with or without caffeine coursing through my veins – desire dictated every beat of my heart.

Luigi was gone so long I wondered if his mother had forbidden his return. The coffee was rising to the top of the pot and filling the tiny room with its bitter dark richness when he returned, releasing the catch on the door which clicked shut behind him.

"At night we add this to our coffee," he said. He poured a generous amount of the sticky fluid into Danielle's fine little cups, handed me one then sat upon the hard unfolded chair. I sat on the bed and feigned interest in the answers he gave to my questions about his family, his work – all the things I would normally ask my students but to which I had never received such eloquent and lengthy response. His voice filled my head, meaningless but mellifluous as the Amaretto that slipped into my blood. I watched as he crossed and recrossed his long legs – his calm voice belied the obvious physical discomfort he found himself in and when he rose to refill my cup I told him to sit on the bed next to me. I believe I told him it was much softer.

"Like you, *bellissima signorina*."

I was suddenly aware of my extraordinary brazenness and of the impropriety of my situation – late, alone, drowsy with liqueur and wearing nothing but my robe and golden slippers. My skin was so sensitised by the possibility that Luigi would soon put his hands upon me that the wool of the robe pricked me at every breath, my nipples rose against the coarse fabric and the cord seemed impossibly tight around my waist. As I held out the cup I could see my hand was shaking, the other one was clutching the edges of the robe together in my lap. Luigi put the bottle on the floor beside him, took the cup from my hand and placed it next to the bottle. He took my other hand and prised my fingers apart, releasing the fabric which parted to reveal my naked legs.

When he rose to stand before me I could see his prick pressing against the faded blue of his jeans. He let go of my hands. I reached out and unbuckled the heavy belt, undid the button and lowered the zip – he had no underwear and his prick burst free. It was thick, chunky almost, and I placed both my hands around it. I looked up at Luigi and saw his wide green eyes gazing down in knowing delight and applied my own insatiable lips to his lovely member. I kissed the tip and ran my tongue along the groove already salty with semen. I licked up and down along its sides and then put as much of it as I could in my mouth. It felt as round as an apple and my lips tingled as the skin stretched. I heard his breathing hard above me and felt his hands on my head then in my hair, stroking my face, running his fingers around my open mouth. Much to my surprise and oral relief, he drew back from me, withdrew his beautiful prick.

I looked up to see him smiling down on me. *"Vieni baciami, cara signorina."*

He helped me stand and wrapped his arms around my waist. My robe was open and the layers of textures were laid upon my skin like treasures in an Indian bazaar – first the metal of the loose buckle, then the coarse denim, the softer cotton of his shirt, then the firm silkiness of his penis, now upright between our bellies, and the tickle of his pubic hair. I raised my arms and encircled his neck, drawing his beautiful leonine head to mine. I kissed him first, gently with closed mouth. He kissed me back, parting my lips with the tip of his tongue. He ran his tongue around them, between them, and I felt it in my cunt, as if his tongue were in my cunt, licking the lips, slipping between them, forcing into the widening hole.

He kissed me and I never wanted him to stop, but I did want more and I risked the momentum by imposing my own. I lowered my arms from around his neck and began the slow and complicated undoing of his shirt buttons. His chest was springy with hair, but I felt the taut hard muscles beneath and his nipples two sharp points.

Without ceasing to kiss me he helped me remove his shirt and it fell to the floor behind him. He then pushed me back upon the bed and I wanted him inside me there and then and I told him in my own tongue to fuck me quickly.

He reached down, pushing my legs apart with his knee. I felt his fingers and then his prick shoved into me so hard. He pushed and pushed and pounded against me and I raised my hips to meet him at every thrust. He felt so huge inside me it was almost unbearable, the scratch of the zip and the roughness of denim, the hard edges of the leather belt all surged into a single exquisite experience where I teetered on the edge of pain. I wrapped my legs around his hips and tore my nails down his back, dug them into his taut buttocks, urging him deeper into me, urging him to come.

And he did, and with such a fury I thought he would split me apart. I felt the pulse of semen from his balls to the tip of his monstrous prick, felt him spurting into me and the rush of semen against my cervix.

He looked down on my wondering face and smiled.

"You didn't come."

"You came enough for both of us and I can still feel you hard inside me."

He bent his arms and lowered himself gently onto my body. He kissed my lips, my eyes, my nose, my chin and slowly he drew out of me, still hard. I felt so empty at his going I wanted to cry. I reached down to take him back into my body, but he pulled back and removed his jeans and his sandals and gestured for me to take off my gown. I could not take my eyes off his rampant prick: "Put it inside me again, please."

He had other plans and lay down on the bed beside me.

"Come and kneel over my face." I straddled his beautiful head and he placed his hands on my hips. "Lower, so I can put my tongue inside you."

Ever obedient I sank until I felt the cool slip of his tongue delving into my cunt. He licked back and forth, lapping the mixture of our juices. He moved my hips gently back and forth, every motion bringing me closer to my orgasm but I didn't want to come just yet. I reached behind me and found his erection, thrusting vainly into the empty air. I hardly had breath to say it but I told him I wanted to kiss him as well. He understood and with an effortless elegance rearranged our bodies.

As I sucked and he licked I recalled the beautiful Indian paintings of lovers performing the complicated couplings of the *Kama Sutra*. I had first seen them in the Oriental section at the Victoria and Albert Museum where the carpet was threadbare with curious feet. Then the lovers had seemed exotic acrobats; now I longed not only for their physical dexterity but for the sonorous jewels that adorned their pale bodies. Luigi's hands circled my ankles like heavy golden clasps, my nipples glowed like rubies and my hair fell around my neck like a silken collar.

I took the ivory column of his penis into my mouth again and again, so wide and long that when the semen rose from the base to its bevelled crown I thought I would never be able to engulf the great tides that broke upon the back of my throat and rushed down into my body – so much semen it poured out of my mouth and into the haze of his pubic hair. I was so distracted by the volume and force of his coming that I was barely conscious of my own, but finally we lay side by side, our faces smeared with milk and honey, utterly sated.

Luigi kissed me and licked his semen from my lips and I tasted myself in the folds of his wings. I remember his arms around me and the strong smell of our sex on our skins and while I was musing on the beauty of this man I feel asleep. I was awakened by the morning pouring in through the open window, a shower of golden light. I flung back the covers that Luigi had obviously lain across me when he left and for a few luxurious moments admired the honeyed richness of my limbs, still languorous with the exertions of last night and ran my hands around my breasts and over my belly. I rose warm and naked, plugged in the kettle and commenced the rituals of the day.

The English Teacher

My days took the form of an Armani suit, loosely structured but well cut, and I wore them with ease and not inconsiderable pleasure. They all began with the mandatory cup of tea and increasingly refined toilette. I would take breakfast in Giuseppe's café and from there make my way to my first lesson. I was a true pedagogue, an itinerant teacher.

Ladrio was the creation of a crooked antipodean, Richard, who ran his business on convenience rather than conviction. This proved to be extraordinarily cost effective. The students did not come to a school – there was none – the teachers went to the students. There were in effect no overheads. Ladrio did not even pay copyright for the teaching method we used, the books were photocopied. The ruse was so obvious I was surprised none of the students ever commented on it, but my boss's wife Susan, a striking pragmatist and our only contact with the mysterious Richard, explained that Italians were the most corrupt people on earth. They did not care for legalities as long as they got a good deal, and they certainly did from Ladrio. The price of the lessons seemed extortionate to us but they were in fact comparable to those of the language schools which had so many overheads that the teachers got a tiny percentage of the hourly rate. We received 50% and our students did not have to leave their offices or shops for one minute.

I travelled the length and breadth of Milan in pursuit of my students' vowels. I used every means of transport from the juddering trams to my high-heeled feet at least once a week when there was a *sciopero* – strike. The equanimity with which these frequent disruptions of routine were greeted amazed me since the Italians were not ones to take even a moment's inconvenience lightly. Queues were simply not acceptable, and having been brought up to wait my turn I often found myself left at the bus, tram or metro stop while the doors squeezed shut on the elegant crowds inside. I would stand astonished as haute couture turned hoi polloi in its frantic bid for a seat. It took many late arrivals and blisters to break the habits of a lifetime but eventually I too threw good manners to the fume-filled wind and pushed and shoved with the smartest.

If the commuters had been waiting what they considered to be an unreasonable length of time they would curse the driver, the system, the government and beat their chests in remorse for the passing of the days when Il Duce made the trains run on time. But when there was a strike these same commuters would simply scan the brief notice – *Sciopero* – attached to the closed grills of the Metro, shrug their padded shoulders and walk to work. Perhaps their calm acceptance was due to the fact that many people who worked in Milan also lived there and the outskirts were not that wide. Moreover, many had cars which they parked with even less concern for the free flow of traffic when they were forced to use them because of the strike. Cars were usually deposited in front of the building the driver wished to enter, whether that building was in a no entry street, no parking zone or a pedestrian area. When there was a strike they were abandoned on tram lines and roundabouts.

I never fathomed the reason why the Milanese accepted the strikes but not the delays. It was not due to socialist tendencies manifesting themselves in sympathy with the strikers, nor to any particular political affiliation because the Italians had none. Their politics were not a matter of who was in power but for how long. I tried on many occasions to discuss the state of the nation with my older students but they were alternately bemused by my interest and bored with my questions – quite simply they did not care. I realised that if they were not the most corrupt nation on earth the Italians were the most amoral – a state, I suppose, which allows for the practice of corruption. From fur coats to foreign policy it was a matter of *lasciare fare*, as long as it did not interfere with what was already being done.

Having suffered the pangs and arrows of outrageous guilt inculcated by a convent school education, I was appalled and then quite admiring of my acquaintances' total lack of opinion on matters that had exercised my young mind and those of my moral mentors for years. Agonising decisions were never made, consciences were never racked – it was simply a matter of practicalities. If they wished to marry in church the affianced had to attend a series of lectures on natural birth control, which they did on the way to buy contraceptives. In spite of the easy availability of such and the illegality of abortion, several of my students had undergone terminations. This they also did with absolutely no sense of guilt and saw no clash between the requirements of their real lives and the unrealistic requirements of their religion. It all seemed so sensible.

Everything was permissible if practical. Wrongdoing was that which did you no good – hence my disinclination to eat meat was suspect because it simply was not clever to deprive the body of what it needed. I was not pale and interesting, I was anaemic and stupid. My horror at Susan's transformation from sundried Aussie to smooth-cheeked Milanesa via the application of placenta was similarly greeted with ridicule – the placenta was from aborted fetuses.

"Surely it is better that they do some good," argued Lina, a student of mine who had given Susan her first capsule of the stuff when in a moment's distress she had told us of Richard's infidelity with his young secretary. Lina attributed this to Susan's crow's feet rather than Richard's lechery and told us the placenta would render the discarded wife the nonpareil of youthful beauty. She opened her left hand and showed us how her palm was free of lines in the centre into which she daily broke the capsule before applying it.

Two weeks later Susan's fate was indiscernible to a fortune teller and her face that of a teenager. The secretary remained in place.

Adultery, Abortion, Abuse of self or others, by soft, hard or liquid drug, in veins or in cafés where 100% proof was downed with espresso before the day was up – the three As were worn with as much panache as Hester's scarlet letter, but with absolutely no fear of eternal damnation.

In my nun-made brand of Catholicism the most important A was Absolution. Everything was forgivable if you felt bad enough about it – the Church Fathers were way ahead of Freud. My Italians however, never felt the need for absolution, they knew they were absolutely right and the Church would catch up sooner or later, but for the meantime they simply got on with it. 'Thou shalt be discreet' was the only commandment ever obeyed and then not to the letter.

It seemed as if everyone had a paramour of sorts, including myself, who did not feel the least guilt when Mrs C took me to her bed – I saw it as something apart from my affair with Luigi, and none of his business. Besides, living amongst the Milanese, guilt seemed a particularly unrewarding indulgence and I learned to take my pleasure honestly. In my classes, many with eloquent and intelligent women like Mrs C who claimed to need conversation practice but who were in fact simply bored, I learnt a great deal about Italian life and European attitudes, so different from those I had hauled with me over the Channel.

The learning process was definitely two-way. I enriched their vocabulary, but all my students enriched my life immeasurably. My favourite was Antonio. He was the nephew of a beautiful man I taught over breakfast in his small but perfectly formed apartment off Via Monte di Pieta while his wife rushed around us attending to her toilette, wandering through the kitchen in various states of dress and undress, continually interrupting the lesson to question her husband on the whereabouts of certain items of her clothing. After five lessons Antonio Senior asked if I would mind his nephew, Antonio Junior, using up the remaining block of hours and though sad to lose sight of his lovely face, I of course agreed.

The nephew was obviously destined to achieve his namesake's good looks and at six had the widest, darkest eyes and the sweetest rosebud mouth that had ever graced a child's face. Moreover, he was quite brilliant. His enthusiasm and ability to absorb the flow of words between us astounded me. It must have been his innocence and consequent trust of me, but he never questioned my pronunciation, my explanations or my demands. He accepted my authority with a graciousness worthy of royalty. I did rather lower myself in his esteem however, when he realised I could not use sign language. His mother was deaf and although she actually spoke in a brutal guttural voice rather than sign to Antonio, he always used his hands as well as his lips to convey his thoughts and needs to her. He was obviously the light of her life and indeed of the whole family, which resided in a huge apartment in the North of Milan.

Unlike the uncle's pad, all black and white and compact, this living space was dark with mahogany and shuttered windows. In the slatted light the bookcases lining the walls of the room where we took our lessons seemed rather threatening and, unusually for me, I was not inclined to pull out every leather-bound volume and read it. My student explained that his grandfather had been a bit of a bibliophile and for the first three years of his life Antonio would be sat in a playpen in the middle of the library floor while his grandfather read out loud between puffs on the thick Havana cigars that killed him.

I had such affection for this child. My heart was light when I lifted the massive gilt knocker and heard the hurried feet thumping and sliding across the wooden floor as he ran to open the heavy door to me every Wednesday afternoon. I also knew a sadness as I listened to the bright chatter and the wonderful stories of a child's voice his mother would never hear. His giggles in the sombre air were like splashes in water, tinkling down into the old lives around him, the lives of his maternal and paternal grandmother and the antique maid who shuffled in with cakes and coffee precisely thirty minutes into every lesson. I do not know if more people lived in the apartment, he never mentioned his father and I did not ask.

Sometimes he would draw pictures and ask me to describe them in English and these pictures were as bright and colourful as his home was dark and old. At the end of such lessons he would always insist on me taking the pictures since, he explained, he had them in his head so I could put them on my wall. I have them still, not on my wall but treasured between the leaves of a book I love well. Antonio is in my head and my heart a child forever.

I grew very fond of all my students, many of whom I saw several times a week, and I began to take great pride in their progress. From my diffident beginnings I learnt to assert myself and my accent, impose my meanings and pronunciation on so many I felt as if I were teaching them not so much the Queen's English as my own particular brand. If Megan's students were recognisable for their ve-ge-taables mine could quote the odd line from Shakespeare, and all the children knew where Narnia was. (This was a world as yet uninhabited by Harry Potter.) I explained my use of unorthodox learning tools by citing the universal, nay eternal, truths of Shakespeare and the weather in the wardrobe. Susan was sceptical, knowing that I had no enthusiasm for the dreary series of questions and answers 'The Method' demanded, but she was content with the incoming fees and left me to my own devices.

Just once I was given a student whose vocabulary I never improved, but who taught me so very much that my understanding of Italian moved from the pedestrian to the poetic. Whether Susan gave me to him because she thought me the most capable of her teachers or the most gullible, then I did not know. Now, of course, I do.

Word Play

Mr Parola was a dazzlingly dapper man, all of 5'6 and a veritable human dynamo. Astoundingly successful and consequently one of the richest men in Milan, he had created a design studio from which he pronounced on the shape of things to come. The curve of the new season's sofa, the height of the dining chairs, the cloth in which they should be covered and whether the lighting should be up or down, wall bound or hanging from a textured ceiling. It was all so alien to me then and so beautiful. The very blackness of the metal lamp stands was dramatic, anglepoise was just that, the epitome of elegance. I marvelled at the clarity of the lines, the voluptuousness of the curves – it was couture for living space.

Yes, I was a great admirer of Mr P. Having seen many of his designs in *Vogue* and *Casa* I was already in awe of him before we met, before I entered his elegant office off Monte Napoleone. You turned left at Valentino's and right through an elaborate iron gate into a walled courtyard. In its centre was a white marble fountain tinkling icy water in which I often rinsed my hot and sticky hands before pushing the immaculate brass plates on the smoked glass doors into Sailor. It is only looking back that I make the connection between Mr P's blazer and the nautical name of his company – it might have been coincidental, but he only ever wore the blazer with the white shirt, charcoal grey trousers, black slip-ons and a dark tie. He was ship shape and shiny from his balding pate to his Fratelli Rossetti slip-ons. His gold rimmed spectacles sparkled, the gold buttons on his navy blazer gleamed, his white shirt glowed and his heavy gold Rolex glistened on his wrist, above a gold ring with a twinkling diamond that he wore on the pinkie of the left hand. Even his teeth shone beneath the neat moustache.

Of course I was not quite so awed by the diminutive reality, but his gracious Italian greetings and open smile quite charmed me. It was only when we began our first lesson together, his twentieth, that any discrepancy in all but our height and financial status was eradicated. It is an observation I have made frequently since, that being brilliant in one particular sphere does not guarantee any enlightenment of other worlds. The man had a brain for business, an eye for fine lines and a strong sense of colour, but socially he was beyond the pale and he had what could only be described as a mental block on English.

Yet I should not perhaps pronounce on his linguistic ability, as it became obvious to me that he had little intention of learning the language. Although he was aware of the commercial benefits of easy discourse with foreign businessmen, in the course of several meetings scheduled for the middle of our lesson hour I watched him use his translator and myself as devices to interrupt, distract and sometimes so completely confuse the buyers that he got exactly what he wanted from them by pretending he didn't understand what they wanted of him. The translator was invariably a pretty young thing, pulled from the pool of pretty young female things that filled the office, all of them long, slim, dark-eyed (hair colour various) and under twenty.

He could have his pick of any of these girls and when I entered Sailor for the first time they must have placed bets on how long it would take Mr P to bed me. Not that I was so very attractive, but I was female and my blonde hair and English origin lessened the odds dramatically. The extraordinary thing to me then as now was that my feelings, or lack of them, were never of any interest to Mr P or his employees. Had they ever heard it, they would all have affirmed that universally acknowledged truth that a single man in possession of a good fortune must be in want of a wife, the logical extension of which being that any single woman without one must want him as a husband. I can say, hand on heart, that though he was as arrogant as a Darcy I never for one moment contemplated him as a husband or lesser consort, and so became the most desirable woman to pass through his portals.

His rudeness was legendary, indeed he had elevated the verbal put-down to an art form, but to me he was always polite, apologising profusely for his bad English in impeccable and sonorous Italian, and so disarmingly charming. Like every Italian, he complimented me on my dress sense. I soon learnt to disregard such flatteries – it was habit, like the English mentioning the weather. He told me I was beautiful and sometimes leant across the desk to stroke my blonde hair. I was not unduly surprised by this gesture; my women students often did the same thing.

"*Ma lei è bionda? Veramente bionda? Come sono morbidi i suoi capelli,*" and so forth.

Moreover he had a patrician air, suitable for a man in his position and so much older than me. I should have been alerted by Susan's questions after my third lesson with him.

"How is Mr Parola? Is he all right with you? You mustn't take him too seriously you know."

"He doesn't seem to take his English lessons too seriously. Perhaps he needs someone more experienced, but frankly Susan, it isn't worth his money – he will never learn."

"But it's such a lot of money Julia, and he always pays for twenty five lessons in advance. He didn't get on well with Jack. It was Jack who suggested you might have better luck with him, he thought you'd have more patience. Besides, he wanted a girl. I know you are new to this but I told him you were our best teacher and if he likes you he'll pay now for another 25 to guarantee your services."

This was very unusual: Ladrio charged so much no one ever paid for more than ten lessons at a time. The following day Susan told me that not only had Mr P paid for fifty lessons, he wanted five a week, at the end of every working day. He liked me.

He took his time – he could afford to, we spent so much of it together. I would sometimes grow frustrated, weary at the constant repetition of such simple phrases that he seemed wholly incapable of pronouncing. He would smile, his eyes bright and wicked behind his glasses, delighted at my distress, and say *"Ancora bella Giulia, ancora."* I insisted that it was immoral to take the man's money when he obviously had no aptitude for the language, but Susan told me to be patient, the penny would drop sooner or later, and it did.

It took about thirty lessons. He was late and I sat in front of his desk, marking the homework of my previous students. I did not hear him enter. Everything in the building was smooth and quiet, the doors did not even disturb the air as they swung effortlessly back and forth. I did not know he was in the room until I felt his hand on my hair. He caught it on the nape of my neck, lifted and twisted it through his fingers, the other hand he put on my throat, slipping it under my pearls.

"Come vorrei mettere i tuoi capelli tutt'intorno al mio cazzo."

I did not dare move my head for fear of losing my hair or my pearls. I sat still and silent until he released his hold on both. By the time he had walked around to the other side of the desk I had repossessed enough of myself and my *sang froid* to offer a cool greeting: "Good afternoon, Mr Parola, how are you?"

"Yes, yes," he said and sat down. He was smiling and looked so inoffensive I could not believe he had actually just voiced a desire to wrap my hair around his prick. He had never touched my skin before, but I had seen him touching the naked arms and knees of his harem and hoped he had merely forgotten himself or that I had misheard.

"*Ma oggi, tu sei ancora più bella di prima.*"

I was concerned at the sudden change from the polite *lei* to the familiar *tu*.

"*Forse è perche le tue bellissime tette sono scoperte – si possono immaginare dentro la mia bocca.*"

There had definitely been a change in tack. I recognised '*tette*' from one of my many linguistic errors. Having exclaimed in Italian at the beauty of the sparkling snow on the rooftops in the mountains where Megan and her married lover had taken me, my hysterical friends explained the difference a vowel makes: '*tetti*' was roofs, '*tette*' was tits, however you saw them – covered in snow or in kisses. I was not mistaken this time. Mr P had made no slip of the tongue unless it was across my breasts, which he had just imagined in his mouth.

I put my head down to hide my burning cheeks. Should I confront him? Should I walk indignant from the room? Yet to do so would mean admitting that I understood his obscenities and was therefore complicit in their generation. I decided to play stupid, trusting in a show of innocence, giving him the opportunity to back off, if not apologise, without any loss of face. I asked him to turn to the third lesson for the third time and we spent the inevitable hour in innocuous verbal angst. I had made the right decision, and not a naughty word was heard.

The next day, Mr P was waiting for me, pacing his spacious office. When I was seated he turned his back on me to survey the courtyard on the other side of the glass wall. Whether the silence was tactical or necessary for the formulation of the following English words I could not tell.

"Julia, today we have discuss, no?"

"Well, we can either discuss something, have a discussion or have a conversation, yes."

He turned to me with the most beatific of smiles, sat behind his desk and said, "*Come vorrei chiavarti.*"

'*Chiavare*' – an amusingly graphic verb, meaning to put the key in the lock, one of the many Italian words for fuck, another being '*scopare*', to sweep, endearingly domestic but the erotic concept eluded me.

In my embarrassment I found a moment's anger and snapped back, "If you wish to have a conversation with me Mr P, it will have to be in English, and I suggest we talk about something in particular, it could even be relevant – how about your house? I assume it's a showcase for your work."

He looked bemused, perhaps by my vocabulary, perhaps a little hurt at my response to what he no doubt considered a compliment, so I asked a few direct questions. He fared better than I expected, even seeking to illustrate his home with pictures in a magazine devoted wholly to his magnificent palazzo halfway between Milan and Brescia, to which he invited me for eats and vino. I ignored his invitation but offered my compliments on the decor. I would have loved to visit such a place, to be its cherished guest, but I wondered if the entrance fee would be a good tupping from the diminutive Lothario.

"*Basta*, I tell you my home, you tell me your home."

So I did, and in the telling felt the sadness of separation from all things familiar, the comforts of childhood, the cushions of the past. I recalled the fabrics, the colours, the scents of my parents' beautiful Surrey house, the long lawns and the flowerbeds bursting with my mother's devotion.

"*Ne senti la mancanza, no?*"

"Yes, I miss them very much. I miss my home, but I do love Italy, I love being here."

"I love you here."

I looked up to see Mr P looking back at me – no irony in his soft voice, no dirt in his eyes. He removed his glasses and placed them on the desk and smiled. He walked up to the window and pulled a metal beaded cord which operated the slatted blinds. They swished across the glass wall and with a twist of the perspex rod at the side of the cord they turned to form a wall of white. He walked behind me to the door which he locked, and on his way back to the desk drew a comfortable chair from the wall to the centre of the room.

"*Siedeti, cara Giulia*".

He gestured towards the chair, and I did as I was bade and sank into the plush pale green upholstery. Mr P drew my vacant chair opposite and sat in it. Now I was bemused and not a little apprehensive. He spoke in Italian.

"I want you to listen. I want you to watch, you don't have to do anything. I have listened to your lovely voice for so many hours now I hear you talking to me in my sleep, in my dreams. I lie in my bed at night with the balcony doors open and the curtains billowing in the soft breeze and in the whisper of leaves I hear your voice. And do you know what I do? I throw back the sheet and I lie there naked and I let your voice cover me and caress me."

While delivering this soliloquy Mr P was staring straight at me, holding my eyes so fast that I could not look away. His voice was unnervingly mesmeric, so soft and low. He knew I understood every word of the most beautiful Italian I had ever heard – an idiot in my language, he was a poet in his own. He held my gaze but I was aware of his hands moving across his waist, I heard the unbuckle of his Gucci belt and the slick unzipping.

"I hear your voice but I must imagine your presence. I take my prick in my hands and I feel it is your hands that surround me, your fingers that clasp me, your palms that move up and down my taut flesh. I imagine your lovely head lowered over my groin, your golden hair flowing over my belly. I hold my breath as I wait for your lips to touch gently to the tip of my aching prick. I feel your lips part and your tongue tip slip along the groove, already weeping with desire for your mouth. Then you open your mouth and my prick is in that warm wet haven. You suck me hard and you move your head up and down, my prick touches the back of your throat but you keep on sucking. Your fingers circle the base of my prick, you feel it growing larger, you feel the tightening of my balls, we both feel the throbs, feel them stronger and faster and then the pulsing as the semen courses along it and spurts out and into your waiting mouth, fills it and flows down your throat, down your chin, down your neck and between your breasts. I lift you up and you kiss me pouring the salty fluid back into me, into my mouth and I lick it from your chin, from your neck and from between your breasts."

I knew he had his prick in his hands, they were still and the glistening tip showed above them. I had not taken my eyes from his but I sensed his erection and in the midst of my horror I sensed my own desire, not for the man before me but for the rich, voluptuous voice and the desirable woman of whom he spoke.

"Don't speak. I can hear your voice in my head. Like the semen flowing from my prick, like the juice flowing from your cunt, it is flowing over me like honey and I wish a thousand tongues to lick it. I wish to lick you but I can't. I want to touch you, but I can't. You must touch yourself for me. I sit here opposite you day after day and I watch your glossy pink mouth and think of my prick in it. I look at your breasts and think of my hands upon them. Let me see them. Undo your blouse."

The room had become so silent. I could hear no outside noise, no phones ringing, no voices, not even the tinkling of the courtyard fountain. All I heard was my own heart pounding in my chest which heaved painfully in its effort to draw breath.

"Don't worry. I won't touch you. I just want to see your breasts. I want you to touch them for me."

I undid the buttons of my pink silk blouse, all of them, and parted the fabric so my exquisite pink bra was exposed. Mrs C had gifted me a veritable trousseau of lingerie.

"Take off your blouse. No one will enter. Take off your bra, as I have dreamt of doing for so long. I lift those frail ribbon straps from off your shoulders, I lift those heavenly spheres from the fragile cups and I feel them full of desire and your nipples grow hard between my fingers and I bring my head to your breasts and take each crimson nipple in my mouth, rolling it between my teeth, flicking it with my tongue. I can see your nipples growing hard. Touch them for me, show me how they feel."

I felt completely safe in my half-naked state, and curiously free. His sonorous voice reverberated in my head and along every nerve of my body. It filled me like a feast, engorged my senses, swelled my breasts. I placed my palms upon my upraised nipples, then slid my fingers over them and around them. I ran my fingertips around the darkening aureoles and widened the circle until I had caressed each entire breast, so soft but full. I wanted to squeeze them, to suck them, to shove them into Mr P's mouth. But he sat still and implacable before me, his hands still in his lap, still around the miraculous column of his penis.

"Lift up your skirt."

I pulled it over my hips so it garlanded my waist.

"Take off your knickers."

I raised my buttocks from off the chair and slid the scant covering down to my ankles and over my shoes onto the floor. The material of the chair was coarse but not uncomfortable, and only added to the confusion of sensations.

"I want you to put your hands on your thighs. Feel how rich they are, how magnificent. I want you to imagine them around my neck. Stroke them as I would stroke them. Feel my hands upon you, move them up high, higher to the curls of your cunt. Feel my fingers stroking the hair, parting the hair, slipping in."

I did as I was told and having caressed my way upward, I felt the juice flowing out of me and into the soft hair which seemed to part like waves under my fingers. I had a moment's shame when I heard Mr P draw a sharp breath but then I closed my eyes and abandoned myself to the experience. I slipped one, then two, then three fingers deep inside me, drawing them out covered in juice and moving them up to my clitoris which was by now an urgent little bud aching to burst into bloom. I rubbed the bud with my middle finger, the others fluttering like butterfly wings on either side.

"Put your fingers, put your hand inside you."

My free hand had been clutching my right breast, drawing it upward and outward towards Mr P – how I longed for him to come and suck it, knowing that he wouldn't. But he knew how it would feel to take my nipple between his teeth, to flick his tongue over it, to force as much of my flesh into his mouth as possible. Now I slid it down under the waves of my left hand, forcing all four fingers between the wet swollen lips.

"Push them hard inside you, deep inside. Feel the softness, the fullness, the wetness. Feel the deepness up to your womb and imagine that it is my hand inside you, forcing deeper into you. I cannot touch you, but I can look at you and you can feel me. See how your hands are caressing me, wrapped around me while my fingers are in your cunt."

I opened my eyes and looked down into his lap. His hands were moving up and down his erect penis, the head purple with blood and shiny with semen. His voice did not falter as he said, "Don't stop caressing us, go as far as you need. I want you to let go, I want you to come."

I could hardly breathe for the furious feeling in my breast and belly, but my fingers found their own momentum, taking their rhythm from Mr P's hands which moved faster and harder up and down his prick. I heard his breath quicken with mine and watched as the semen spurted out of him and over his hands, over the dark cloth of his trousers. And I too came, the walls of my vagina closing on my four fingers like an anemone. The sensation pulsed through me from my cunt to my breasts and burst behind my eyes in a brilliant white light. I was dazzled, and the light was all around me and I was the light and the light poured down over my body until I shone with sweat.

I became aware of a sound, so low and deep it was like a far thunder, but it was Mr P's voice, "Dearest Julia, don't open your lovely eyes – I have something for you to hear. You are more magnificent in the flesh than you ever were in my dreams, and now I have you in my head I will be able to touch you always, to taste you, to see how your skin pinkens and shines, how your breasts bloom and your cunt swells and flows and I will know the warm depth of your mouth and your cunt.

"When you are away from me you will know I am caressing you always, sucking you, licking you. As you bathe in the mornings imagine my hands running over your body with the warm water. As you smooth the pink across your pretty lips imagine you are touching the moist tip of my penis to them. As you sit down to eat at midday, imagine that you are taking me into your sweet mouth with every morsel of food. As you cross your legs in the classroom, imagine my hand is between them, feel my fingers pushing aside the lace of your knickers and delving into you. As you lie in bed at night think of me in my bed with the sheets thrown back and the breeze on my skin, thinking of you on my skin, my skin in your skin, and as the waves of your orgasm wash over you, imagine my semen spurting out of me and splashing over you and into you. Imagine that forever I will be hard with desire for you, full of desire for you and every night and day, every moment of every night and day I will be caressing you, licking you, kissing you – I will be in you always."

The voice stopped and I was aware of movement. When I was sure he had gone I opened my eyes into the brightness filtering through the slats. Mr P had left a door open into what I had thought was a cupboard but in which I made out a sink and a light reflecting in a mirror above it. My limbs were heavy and I wanted merely to lie upon the soft white rug and wrap myself in it and sleep. But I knew I must leave, and with some semblance of decorum.

The cupboard was a concealed washroom and in it I found all the fragrant necessities for restoring my professional body. The towels were thick and fluffy as a dream and the cologne I rubbed over my hot skin was sharp and sparkling like sunshine to wake me. I could not stem the flow of juice from my cunt and resolved to enjoy the silkiness between my legs. I brushed my hair, retouched my makeup and thought of Mr P as I applied my lipstick. I closed the closet door and walked to his masterpiece of a desk. I knew he could see me, but from where I couldn't imagine.

I opened the English grammar book that lay like an admonition on the walnut surface, removed again my damp pink knickers and placed them between chapters 3 and 4. I unlocked the door to the office of the receptionist who had obviously, like all the other employees, gone home into the milky Milanese dusk, but on her desk was a bright white envelope with my name in curly black letters, next to it a small black oblong box with a pink ribbon to which a card with my name was attached. I picked them up and walked briskly out through the smoked glass doors, past the solitary security guard who bade me good evening and into the cooling air which fell upon my naked cunt like a lover's breath.

Mr P's florid Italian script swept across the page to form the following hurried words:

My dearest Julia

You are a dream from which I never wish to wake, from which I never wish you to wake. I will never meet you again, you will understand why. I will never learn English but we share a language of our own. My hand around this pen is my hand around my penis gorged with the thought of you. Use it well. I caress you always.

Silvano

P.S. I have paid for lessons until your departure – please use your free hours to enjoy yourself as I have enjoyed you.

I still have the gold pen. I used it every day for many years. It added a piquancy to the signing of cheques, but I never did see Mr P again, even when I went for my lessons with a remarkably inoffensive and conscientious young woman in an office on the far side of the courtyard. Not that I ever looked for him. I always walked across that marble space with my eyes firmly fixed on my destination, never tempted to turn my head to the glass wall behind which Mr P must often have stood to watch my hurried passing. But every journey across was charged with sensation. No matter how many layers of clothing lay upon my skin, I would feel them fall from my body until I was naked except for the imagined touch of his hands, which I remember even now.

Skin Deep

I embraced my new life and my emerging persona with the energy and enthusiasm of optimistic youth but I felt a soft sorrow for the old ways, for the child Julia, for the child of my parents and England.

I called home nearly every day – no mean feat then. I had to queue in the telephone exchange at the station to pay for my call and then queue again until a booth became free. I would dial the number like a mantra and like magic there would always be a familiar voice at the other end. I was homesick, but with no ostensible cause. My life was certainly full, the only time I spent on my own was necessary to maintaining a modicum of professionalism by marking papers, setting tests and preparing for the next day's lessons – even this was a pleasant exercise since it was accompanied by neat Cinzano that fractured the ice as I poured it into the tall crystal tumbler.

Socially I had Megan. We met for lunch in various cafés My favourite was at the mouth of the Galleria overlooking the Piazza del Duomo with its confection of a cathedral spindly and white, and where one cappuccino cost more than a meal. We would pose like Milanese wives putting on and off our Ray-Bans, eyeing up the tight arses of the tight-trousered men, discussing the cavortings of the previous night and imagining those to come. My daytime activities I kept to myself.

Occasionally we took a tram to Bar Magenta, famous throughout the city for its sandwiches and its proximity to the refectory of Santa Maria delle Grazie where the faint forms of Leonardo's *Last Supper* can be discerned on the one wall that escaped the bombings of '43. I was disappointed, Megan was dismissive, but we both agreed it was indeed a miracle that it was still there.

We tore pizzas to pieces and downed litres of cheap wine together several evenings a week and to Megan's surprise the kilos simply slid from my carbohydrate-fuelled form and I rarely got drunk. I took to alcohol like a duck to water, and Mrs C had given me a taste for champagne.

In effect I developed what sounded like a perversion – oenophilia, but it never became a need, unlike with my compatriots who thought a good time was had while dribbling in their cups. Megan usually left me behind in the booze stakes and, often too drunk to get home, would pass out on my mattress. On such occasions I would wipe the mascara from her tight shut eyelashes, the sticky gloss from her lips and lie down beside her on the blade of bed she had spared me. In the mornings she would rise without a word, make coffee for herself and sit at the table with her first cigarette. I was always joyful in the mornings and chattered like a child, much to the annoyance of Megan who simply ignored me. I soon learnt with her, as with many other morning miserables, to keep the tunes in my head and the words for a later hour as I made my own tea and prepared for the day.

Megan's second cigarette was lit to pace the application of her mascara. She would take a drag, put the cigarette in the saucer I kept as an ashtray, pick up the magic wand and sweep it over her long but pale lashes; another drag, another coat of black until the cigarette was burned down and stubbed out. The final oral fix was the lipstick. Her wide, full mouth she outlined with a brown pencil and filled in with a column of lipstick the colour of autumn and which, whatever she wore, seemed the right shade for her face and apparel. I watched her with the same reverential fascination I had bestowed upon my mother when I stood as a child at her dressing table, elbows resting on its immaculate glass top, while she daubed the subtlest of hues on her beautiful face, and occasionally on mine when I asked her to.

It was in contemplating her mirrored features and the way the colours accentuated or diminished them that I first experienced the delight of decoration. I have since been made aware of the implications of lipstick, worn by the boy prostitutes of Ancient Rome to advertise their trade in fellatio. I have been scolded for conspiring in the objectification of my sex, but the colours and the creams still delight and I have seen the prostitutes on Corso Garibaldi and I know the magic of maquillage.

Corso Garibaldi was famous for its prostitutes. It was a 24-hour thing – you could find them dunking their brioche in the dawn, munching lunch in the many cafés and meandering through the purposeful crowds that surged along the street from the Castello bus station to the Metro in the evening rush hours.

There were always whores but they differed with the shifts. The early morning ones were scruffy, unkempt and old. They became progressively better- and higher-heeled as the day wore on until by dusk they were positively stunning. No doubt the dark hid a multitude of imperfections but even in the ghastly neon light of the bars they flashed like film stars on my amazed retinas.

It was as if the contents of *Vogue* were walking the street where I ventured to buy my pizza by the metre. The era of the Jerry Hall and Verushka lookalike, they strode past me a master race of models. And oh the glamour of those legs – so long, glossy and smooth, every hair torn from its socket by the laying on and swift removal of hot wax. They ended under tiny skirts cling-filmed to their tight buttocks, their waists clinched in black leather belts with ornate gold buckles. Their magnificent breasts burst forth from breathtaking tops or between unbuttoned blouses; their necks were almost choked in exotic gold bands, velvet ribbons or silky scarves and their heads rose like tropical flowers above.

The makeup was always immaculate, if heavy and rather mask-like. Any personality the whores may have had was eradicated under the pancake and colours of sexual fantasy – deep crimson lips always parted in an intimation of oral sex, cheeks red with the flush of orgasm and eyelids so heavy with black mascarared lashes they had the languor of the sexually sated. The hair was bouffant, often blonde and, I supposed, fake. I looked them up and down in wonder, pinnacles of desirability, teetering on street corners and impossibly high heels attached to their feet by gold or silver straps as thin as spaghetti.

It was the feet that gave them away – they were just too darned big. All their extremities pointed to the male of the species. Their hands, however delicately arranged about their faces, breasts or stroking their stockinged thighs, were over large for the hairless arms and the red nails only drew attention to the thick fingers they graced.

It took a while to read the signs – the necklaces and chokers covering the apple of Adam, the slim hips and pert arses. It would have taken a lot longer if on the way to pizza one evening Megan hadn't made a typically caustic remark on the injustice of "those disgusting pricks on heels" making ten times more per fuck than we made per lesson.

How I admired those boys. If imitation is the greatest form of flattery they paid homage to femininity every time they painted their lips and unbuttoned their blouses. Megan thought them an insult to womankind – I thought them rather magnificent.

Make up blurred the lines between Madonna and whore that are always drawn so boldly in the mother child relationship. The rouge my mother applied to her cheeks was the blush of warmth and modesty, the lipstick rendered her smile even more shiny and wide and her dark lashes had the sweep of angel wings. Was the red on the whore's mouth a parody or a plea?

Watching Megan I saw how wearisome such a ritual could be, how mechanical, but for me it never lost the magic of a new beginning. Every day I would open the jewellery box of my make up and choose the colours to compliment my clothes. I would often end up as painted as the whores and while still living at home my mother would stop me as I went to leave the house, pull out the clean white hanky she always kept up her sleeve and gently wipe the lurid excesses from my eyelids and cheeks.

From my mother and the whores I learnt how appearance can mirror or disguise your inner state, how apparel and painting your face can be a sign of self-respect or the uncomfortable but necessary costume for a role you need to play, the persona, the mask through which you confront and deceive and please the world. From Mrs Corallo, from Italy, I learnt the absolute, self-indulgent joy of dressing for pleasure, from the sense of silk on naked skin to the soft scratch of a net petticoat, and how heavenly the voluptuousness of a velvet skirt and the lustre of pearls.

At first nonplussed, then disturbed by the constant attention of the Milanese to my appearance, I learnt to accept then expect the appraising glances as my dues. My confidence increased with my wardrobe which was swelled by at least one item every Saturday.

Megan would meet me at midday at a designated café where we ate a hearty breakfast, then meandered through the market and its myriad gaudy stalls. Megan was a cynic to the core and had never embarrassed her body with anything psychedelic, floral or made of cheesecloth – she thought my initial clothing more indicative of a confused ingénue than a peace-loving liberal and suggested I burn every item. She was all sharp lines and clean colours and low heels, short hair and discreet jewellery. I knew these things were not endemic to the Welsh valleys and rightly assumed that if Megan could look the part, so could I.

I immersed myself in style, looked around me and asked my students to show me the labels that lay upon their necks like the precious clasps of family heirlooms – soon I could spot a make at fifty paces. I learnt so many new proper nouns and adjectives that I in effect acquired another language, Fashion. It was not difficult but it was necessary to communication since everyone spoke it, thought it and lived it. Even the seasons were heralded in not by a change in the weather but a change in colour, shape and skirt length. The Winter was over when the ubiquitous green coat was replaced by the Burberry mac and the women's furs by three-quarter length jackets of a uniform beige. By some kind accident I had arrived late into Spring, a season I had always welcomed because of the promise of Summer; in Milan it meant that I did not have to fight through a zoo of dead animals whose fur invariably matched the hair colour of its wearer.

The names of designers became as familiar to me as those of my family and although I could not actually afford to buy from their shops I bought good imitations. My students were not fooled and occasionally suggested I save up to buy a "real Valentino," or try one of the younger and more affordable new designers as an Armani jacket would no doubt prove to be a good investment. The Italians, and especially the Milanese, invested in their appearance in the way the British invested in property – they didn't take out mortgages, they opened wardrobes.

Perhaps their obsession with appearance was the inevitable end of the fresh, bright beginnings of the Renaissance aesthetic, once a fountain of beauty now a puddle of meretriciousness where vanity is spawned. Perhaps their desire for uniformity was borne of a terror of individuality, their slavish devotion to the dictates of fashion a mark of Fascism in this monumental city where the state buildings bore the fading scars of Il Duce's name with the pride of war wounds. Soon I did not care for such philosophical profundities and learnt to skim across the surface of this stagnant pool of decadence with the grace of a dragonfly.

I saw myself reflected in the glass-fronted shops of Monte Napoleone, growing more like the mannequins in their splendid costumes, becoming svelter and sleeker, shedding the pounds along with my clogs and inhibitions. Having spent my entire adolescence searching for an inner meaning I began to enjoy my skin. Having battled my way to the sanctum of my soul I became aware of the temple that contained it and gave my body the reverence it so richly deserved. Every time I lifted my breasts into the increasingly finer lace cups of my brassiere and slipped the ribbons that held them over my shoulders, every time I stepped into the satin sheath of my knickers, I felt the hands of my lovers upon me. I felt them drawing the fragile items of clothing down as I drew them up. I could recall that feeling throughout the day, and if memory dimmed I could revive it every evening with the dazzling sensation of skin on skin.

My sex life was not only full but bursting at the seams, the only limits were those on my body and my imagination. I often wandered around Milan in a daze, the ground falling from under my feet, my belly on fire and my womb contracting in spasms of remembered desire – the images that filled my head of others filling my body were more inebriating than any drug and I would sway from the straps on the tram, aware of the scandalised eyes on my shaven armpits (only the *travestiti* on Corso Garibaldi shaved their underarms). Sated I was certainly, but not satisfied. My sex life was for the most part skin play, surfaces like light on water, like neon flashing on the painted night faces, like the flames of candles flickering over my naked form. All intercourse was of the flesh.

My conversations with Mrs C were always in the context of her boudoir. She had a great affection for me but it took the form of post-coital tendresse. We were lovers but only for a few hours a week, we never socialised. In fact I did not socialise with any of my lovers, never strolled hand in hand, never sat down to eat on either side of a candlelit table, never passed a entire day in their exclusive company. I was lonely, I missed the intimacy of a shared past, of memories that others could refresh for me instead of striving to envisage.

Luigi came close to relieving the dull pain of my departing girlhood. My desire for him seemed to obliterate all other longings when we were together, which we were most nights. In Danielle's apartment I slept more deeply than ever before, my dawn face was creased with smiles and my whole body warm with Luigi's night-long embrace. But he would leave as soon as the sunlight touched him, unlacing himself from my body with a kiss, dressing and departing quickly and silently.

At some point we must have made a tacit arrangement to proceed in this way. I worked long days and Luigi was very vague about his source of income, saying that he was mostly employed by a very wealthy businessman as a go-between in various dealings. Moreover, he seemed to come and go from the family apartment with the freedom of a paying guest, returning only for food and clean clothes when needed. This was of course how all young Italians treated their homes and whether his mother knew of his visits to my abode I neither knew nor cared If she disapproved it never showed when I passed her, albeit rarely, in the courtyard or greeted her at the lift door.

Luigi would arrive around midnight, I was usually in bed with a glass of chilled wine and a book. The wine was always *Pinot de Pinot*, a white wine so fine that when it touched your palate it evaporated, leaving only a fragrant cool air to traverse your tongue and throat; the book was *La Divina Comedia*, a gift from Mrs C.

I had asked her what I should read to improve my Italian and at our next lesson she gave me a parcel from Mondadori in the Galleria. I opened it to find all three volumes – *L'Inferno, Il Purgatorio* and *Il Paradiso*, bound in suitably firey red leather. Daunted at the prospect of reading the whole thing and knowing enough of Italian literature to understand that Dante's masterpiece was not, in spite of its title, a barrel of laughs, nor was his language the sort I could use in the local osteria, my thanks were polite rather than enthusiastic.

Mrs C smiled, sensing my reservations, and took *L'Inferno* from me and opened it, but she did not look at the page.

"*Nel mezzo del cammin di nostra vita*... In the middle of the journey of our life.... Ah, *cara Giulia*, you are only at the beginning, you have such a long way to go. I gave you this book not for the language, you speak well enough. I gave you this because it teaches you the most important thing about my people – we exist only for passion, to describe it and excite it and to feel it. We Italians, we have a passion for everything from making love to making coffee."

I was too young to laugh at the overt propaganda, did not then know that the Americans would soon overtake the Italians as purveyors of coffee, so I listened, with respect and affection.

"Dante wrote the *Comedia* and *La Vita Nuova* because he had a passion for Beatrice and although he wrote as a Christian he was still so close to the roots of his religion, to paganism, that his Beatrice is Venus, the goddess of human and divine love. He writes of unrequited love and of falling in love. I do not think you have yet fallen in love and I hope you have time to simply enjoy before you suffer such a terrible passion as Dante's. My husband gave me this book when we first met, when I was very young, and we read every word together."

Mrs C's education of me was usually more practical, the emphasis being on Italian couture, culture, cuisine and sexual technique. Rarely did she philosophise, but I realised she was telling me something important, something I did not understand and would not for a while to come. If the book was the key I would keep it safe until I found the right door. In the meantime I read it out loud to Luigi and if he was not interested in the war of the Guelfs and Ghibellines he never let me know. His indulgence of my nascent romanticism was complete, albeit fostered by his patriotism – the Italians have a deep pride in their heritage and a reverence for their teachers, of whom Dante is considered one of the greatest.

Luigi interrupted me only once – when I was reading about the swirling shades tempted into adultery by the story of Launcelot and Guinevere. He took the book from me and slid it under the bed while reciting the plangent words of poor Francesca, "*He who shall never be parted from me trembling kissed my mouth. The book was a go-between and that day we read no more.*"

Impressed by my lover's erudition and the extent of his erection I succumbed to his kisses.

For the most part he lay gently beside me, often twining his fingers in the soft gold curls that covered my cunt, always smiling as I stumbled over the words of an antique Italian only a Florentine could have pronounced with any degree of proficiency, and filling my glass which became a magical goblet I could never drain. When the bottle was empty and the canto finished he would undress and make love to me and we would fall to sleep. Sometimes I would stay awake and watch him, listening to him breathe, catching the warm air above his parted lips in my fingers, touching my fingers lightly to his face, not wishing to wake him but hoping I would.

Once when running his hands up and down my skin he asked me what I looked like with my clothes on and I was astonished to realise that he had never met me in any other than a state of near or total undress or outside of the apartment. I think we both knew that we could only be together in this tiny room, but I told him to come at nine the following evening and I promised to be less suitably attired.

I prepared a feast of cool fresh food. With an altruistic shudder I laid the slivers of raw red meat like the petals of a fleshy rose around the huge, white and well-scrubbed platter I had borrowed from the concierge. I found a strange peppery lettuce I had never tasted before and drenched it in olive oil and balsamic vinegar and sprinkled pine kernels over the glossy verdure. The cheese ranged from soft white mozzarella to grainy Parmigiano and included what the vendor had called "*un caprice*" – matured in caves full of aromatic mushrooms, this cheese was speckled with black truffles which cost more per kilo than gold. The fruit was piled precariously on the largest plate I could find and the crystal glasses in the candlelight reflected their colours like precious gems. The crockery was scant but Danielle was a romantic soul – there was an abundance of crystal and the two candlesticks were of exquisite blue Murano glass.

Luigi was uncharacteristically besuited and he was so handsome I took the greatest pleasure in just looking at him. His strong features were ever more magnificent in the candlelight, his thick golden lashes shadowing his emerald eyes. I too had chosen my apparel with care, aware that every item would be appraised and removed. I had even strapped the stilettos with diamante heels to my walk-weary feet, but like Cinderella I knew I could have danced all night. Instead we waltzed through our lives, brief as they were at that time.

Luigi told me of his childhood in the city and I evoked my sunny English upbringing, cloudy only with the Catholic guilt inculcated in my teenage years by the Sisters of the Bleeding Hearts. Having made us believe we were capable of anything, that our sex was not a hindrance, the Sisters sought to contain the powers they unleashed in their young charges with an overwhelming sense of responsibility. They neverthless rarely suceeded in reigning us in and, dangerous women themselves, invariably raised armies of fully breasted Amazons, none of whom entered their order.

Luigi, raised from birth a Catholic, had never experienced the guilt of being a woman in a religion that sanctified redeemed whores and worshipped virgin mothers. The martyrdom of Christ, his Madonnas and his Magdalens, were as familiar as wallpaper to Luigi, and as one-dimensional, part of the interior design of his traditional Italian home.

Many Milanese had discarded the icons and images along with their heavy wooden dressers, huge dining tables and ornately framed landscapes, replacing them with steel and pine and abstract canvases – sharp lines on the white walls of their airy apartments. Luigi's mother however, was from the South and when she married Luigi's tall fair father brought with her not only her mental but her inherited furniture – magnificent mahogany pieces and baroque saints – by way of a dowry.

Luigi was surprised that I considered myself a victim of guilt in any way, my lovemaking was so joyous, my delight in my body and his so complete. Guiltless and guileless himself, he couldn't understand that my need for romance was to justify what I feared was a superficial lust.

The Sisters had acknowledged human nature, and they did not approve. They accepted that lust was extant but only because the world was imperfect, fallen. Looking at Luigi I knew they were wrong. The angels were walking the earth and one folded me nightly in his wings.

Santo Spirito

We were well into the Summer when Danielle asked if he might talk to me after the lesson, about his friend's apartment. The tears sprang instantly to my eyes and quivered against my lashes the whole hour, blurring the page and my attention. It had always been at the back of my mind that I would one day have to vacate the lovenest which had in effect become mine, my magic chamber where every night my Prince Charming came to kiss me to sleep. As the weeks then the months passed by and Danielle had not mentioned his friend I had hoped that he had given up his mistress. What I could not foresee was that he might find another, or as Luigi's mother had intimated, the apartment might be put once more to more lucrative use.

Danielle was so embarrassed at having to ask me to leave I think we both thought I was doing him a favour by endeavouring to vacate the apartment by the end of the week. He softened the blow by telling me of an acquaintance who had an empty room off Via Brera. He gave me her number and again apologised – I realised he had put off this moment for longer than he should have, possibly incurring more than a mistress's wrath, and I wondered if the pressures on him were as much criminal as carnal.

I have often been amazed at the occurrence of coincidence in my life, the chance meeting, the lucky break – fate? Or a fiction we write on looking back, on trying to understand the course of events? If I had not returned to Via Zingara in my lunchbreak, anxious not to waste any moment away from my soon to be gone haven, I would never have known. I can't say that it made it easier. Every time I walked through the Brera or Ambrosiana it was Luigi's face that stared loftily from the canvases, his Renaissance nose and heavy lidded eyes, and the subtle smiles of angels that hinted at the sardonic. In every handsome man I saw Luigi. In every handsome man I see Luigi, I see his eyes in the green of the grass and the trees and the emeralds Alexandros gave me. With Luigi I came dangerously close to falling in love, but only close.

It seems so obvious now, so trite, the notion of the cankered rose. If I'd never known would it have made any difference? I think not The time had come to leave my ivory tower and my dream Prince, and yet the awakening seemed unnecessarily rude as I lifted my heavy legs up the steps from the Metro and walked into the hot light of the public gardens.

In the heat the stench of urine from the junkies who slept on the steps was so strong it followed me up into the green like an intimation of Hades in the Garden of the Hesperides. Were the young people sat on the ground around me shooting up free spirits, the damned, or spoilt brats?

The sight no longer shocked me but it still dragged up deep fears. Drugs were the Devil's work in the Convent where even aspirin were begrudgingly handed out with a harrumph. My schoolmates thought themselves wicked if they managed to take a drag on a cigarette without coughing blood, but the Sisters did their duty. They trod a very thin line between terrifying us and tempting us to seek out the evil pills and powders. They told us they were hearts of darkness into which we should never look, but we were forced daily to confront the flaming hearts in the midst of the ripped torsos of Jesus and Mary: hearts girt with thorns and dripping blood for us for sinners. We took a bad trip daily down the corridor where the garish busts hid like bogeymen in dark alcoves. Their horror for us would perhaps have lessened had we been able to see their remarkable similarity to those psychedelic portraits of Bob Dylan and Janis Joplin in the throes of chemical ecstasy.

There were of course drugs to be had outside the Convent walls. The inmates of the local asylum I visited weekly as part of the Sisters' community work traded their prescriptions on their days out in the Church Hall with a sixth former from the local grammar school. They knew him as Simon. He gave them money which they lost on the horses or pissed away in booze, or he would swap them their tablets for his powder, no doubt cut with chalk from the blackboard. These tragic maniacs were so rattled with pills I could not discern the effects of the medicinal as opposed to the recreational. None of it seemed much fun.

I met my first real junkie at a party I had been taken to by a rather *avant garde* girl called Jill who wore green nail varnish and non regulation knickers to school. The Sisters either considered her beyond redemption or knew her time with us was too short to wage a campaign and did not attempt to remove either, much to our envy since even clear varnish was forbidden us and black underwear seemed so much more daring than navy blue. She never wore her hat or gloves and on the train home would pull a long green feather boa from her satchel and wrap it round her gabardined shoulders. I once asked if I could stroke it and she let me wear it all the way home.

The partygoers were rather ordinary in comparison to my companion. She was wearing little else besides a new pink boa and a pair of terrifyingly high and heavy platform clogs. I was feeling very fashionable in my hot pants and halter neck, and Jill had lent me her green boa which tickled my nose more than any male's fancy. I remember vividly the sense of missing the joke in the fug of dull conversation with dulled intellects – apart from Jill and myself, everyone was stoned. The excitement at being at a grown up party soon abated and I asked an obviously bored Jill if we might leave and go to one of the clubs she was always talking about. She gave me a kind if patronising look and said none of them was open until after the hour she had assured my mother I would be home.

Our discussion on possible other venues was interrupted by an horrific howl. It came from our host. He had locked himself in the bathroom for such a time that there was a queue on the stairs and someone who knew better had scaled the back of the house in an attempt to break in through the bathroom window. I don't know whether it was his mountaineering friend or the host himself who finally opened the door to reveal a manbeast on all fours shrieking at the moon, the music, his guests and the pain on which he was impaled.

"Bad trip," muttered a boy at my side.

It seemed more like a descent into Hell pursued by the Furies as he scrabbled on the landing while his friends held him down and some Harpy held aloft a syringe she had recovered from the lino floor, screaming "you stupid bastard," again and again, at the howling, hurting beast.

Jill took my arm and led me out into the street. She didn't let go of me until she had found us a taxi and dropped me at my door.

"I'm sorry babe, they're all fucking crazy, and so boring. Next time we'll go to the flicks."

We did. It was *Midnight Cowboy* and I was depressed for days afterwards.

The other girls in my class were either too jealous or frightened to be associated with Jill but I was drawn to her brightness and her difference and we became unlikely friends. I took her home for tea and she gave me Jean Genet to read. I didn't understand the mechanics of homosexuality, so she told me about buggery and fisting and I experienced my first visceral clutch – pain and sex seemed the oddest of bedfellows to me even then and De Sade, subsequent gay friends, Genet's Lady of the Flowers pierced with Seven Sorrows never persuaded me otherwise. The door to Samois was closed to me from that time but Jill gave me the map to other worlds I have wandered in with pleasure for years.

I met Darling Daintyfoot and Divine on Corso Garibaldi, fluttering their arses and eyelashes at every passing fancy. In Lourdes I attended the voluptuous masses those queens so adored. Pagan ceremonies where gold chalices are raised to reverent lips and arosoirs baptise the faithful with fragrant water while gold censers envelop them in a heady haze of frankincense that on inhaling seems to stop the heart. In Genet I sensed the beauty in corruption, in Luigi I knew it. My beautiful angel was fallen. Lucifer practised the black art of drug dealing.

That midday I walked briskly from the stinking exit across the grass towards a familiar shape. Luigi was so tall and in the sunlight his fair hair was golden. I recognised the pale linen jacket he had shrugged across his shoulders as he left my room that morning. I was so surprised to see my lover in the daytime and in the open air I did not think to call to him and slowed my pace to enjoy the view.

He too had been walking purposefully, towards a small group of casual young men lounging on the ground. As he approached he raised his hand in greeting, then strode into their midst and crouched down. Several of the men looked around them; Luigi did not but proceeded to empty his pockets onto the grass. I reached the edge of the group and in response to the murmurs Luigi finally raised his head. He said nothing, but indicated that he knew me with a nod to the surrounding youths who stared me up and down with a disdain I had not yet experienced in this voyeuristic city.

"*Chi e?*"

"*Un'amica.*"

I stood silently by as Luigi handed out small packets of white pills and white powder. Not a word was spoken. I was too scared to move but from under my lowered eyelids saw that all around me was a park full of mothers and children and lovers and idle youth, not one *carabiniere* was near.

Done with his dealing Luigi took me by the arm much as Jill had done several years before and led me from the circle and back to the path.

"Why did you follow me? You only had to ask."

My eyes were burning with the brightness and tears and my voice sounded so young and frightened I could not believe it was mine: "What were you doing?"

"What do you think? I'm a dealer, the best."

"Do you take them?"

He looked at me with a disdain akin to that of the young men as he pushed up his jacket sleeves and undid the cuffs of his creased white shirt. He exposed the underside of his golden forearms, the ridges of veins running blue and uninterrupted from wrist to elbow.

"I thought you knew my body well enough to know that there isn't a mark, not even a pin prick on it, apart from the half moons your nails leave on my back."

He laughed softly and the eroticism of the image, the memory of his beautiful body over mine, momentarily distracted me from my purpose, then a particularly louche young male sauntered past us with a leer and a few Italian words to Luigi about the pretty young prostitute who was keeping him in at nights.

Luigi did not respond with words but lowered his head and smiled, perhaps in embarrassment, perhaps in genuine amusement at the passing shot of his insalubrious acquaintance – I could not tell. It appeared that I knew very little about this man with whose body and life I considered myself so intimate. I chose to ignore the reference to my alleged profession and returned to my lover's.

"If you don't take drugs Luigi why are you involved in such a filthy business?"

"That's your nuns talking and they talk shit – how do you know it's filthy? How do you know anything? You make love like Messalina but you are an innocent in so many things. Trust me, I never made you take anything did I? Who needs drugs when you have me to, how do you English say? Turn you on."

Here he paused and looked at me with a smugness that I never thought to see on such an artlessly lovely face. Receiving no assurances as to his sexual prowess he shrugged his shoulders and continued: "I provide a service. I deal only with top people, big people. They trust me with their money and I get them the best. I have good connections, my boss is one of the richest men in Milan."

"Then why are you fishing for such small fry as flounder in the cesspits of the park?"

The analogy eluded him but he got the gist.

"This is just pocket money. Anyway, why are you so bothered? You never seemed that interested in my work, it didn't matter, we met to make love, not do business. Or that's what I thought. What did you think I did? Why did you follow me here?"

"I didn't think and I didn't follow you. I have to leave the apartment."

"When? Are the girls coming back?"

The girls, maybe he supplied them, maybe he fucked them, such bitterness in me so suddenly.

"The girls I don't know about, but I have to leave soon."

"I shall miss you, I shall miss you very much. *Ti voglio bene.*"

I want you, I want good for you – *ti voglio bene* – these three words were heartfelt and softened the cruel realisation that Luigi knew our affair could not survive beyond its magic domain. Indeed, that he had no wish that it should.

If he was not quite sincere in the delivery of his wishes I knew I would feel his loss keenly. I had so adored him, his body and his beauty, it gave me joy just to look at him. I had described him so often and so enthusiastically to Megan that she insisted I was blinded by my lust. Once she had questioned me as to the size of his prick. I was well beyond blushing at anything and had simply said, "Huge."

Megan had narrowed her eyes, taken a deep drag on her menthol cigarette and exhaled with a sigh. She ground the half-burnt fag into the saucer (only rarely did she suck them to the tip) and said, "Thought so." And from then on she dismissed my raptures with reference to my gross requirements.

Megan definitely had a point, but Luigi had fulfilled more than my basic needs. Luigi and I had shared pleasure through our bodies, so much pleasure since that first night when we had opened the treasure chest of each other, when my painted toenails had seemed like rubies and his eyes were emeralds and his hair spun gold. He had loved my body; I had loved this man with my body and my heart and my imagination. Did the discrepancy in our feelings turn the gold to dross? Had I wanted him so much more than he wanted me, or had we both been complicit in an illicit plundering, the spoils of which we would have to return to the rightful owners, neither of which was ourselves?

Was the sudden disappointment I felt due to an indoctrined indignation as to his profession or a realisation that I really had been living in a fantasy of my own making, not his?

I looked up at him now and his eyes were tight against the brightness. He looked older and I knew that the sun on my face was not as kind as the candlelight – we had both awoken into a crueller day.

We walked in silence across the park and the busy road, but when we reached Via Zingara Luigi told me he must go. I smiled what I hoped looked like Mrs C's smile and said nothing. He kissed the top of my head and said he'd be back around midnight, then he turned out of the tunnel and into the light and Buenos Aires. I watched his long straight back and the hair that fell down onto his broad shoulders until the crowds and the traffic took him in.

I knew I never wanted to see him again and I was filled with a distinct but undefinable fear. Was it the drugs? I was of course scared, of the dirt, the stale piss, the gulleys of empty veins, the ridges of blocked veins, and the way the stars could turn to blades that sliced your flesh and gouged out your mad eyes. We had not heard of AIDS then, but what I saw was enough.

I am not scared now – they have no mystery, no horror for me now, Luigi's pills and powders. I know the rich languor they can induce and the magical distance they span between reality and the unreal. But in the park it had seemed so tawdry, so unfitting – I could have imagined Luigi walking on water before I saw him trading in bloody diamond earrings and the gold crosses of babies.

I called Danielle from Giuseppe's café and at the end of the day I returned to pack my belongings in the suitcase I kept under the bed with the fur coverlet. As the cage shuddered down the lift shaft I felt tears on my cheeks and tasted salt in my mouth. I did not want to leave my enchanted tower but my Prince Charming was a dealer not in dreams, but in drugs – to have the face of an angel and the income of a pimp seemed so grossly unfair I wondered if the world would ever seem right again.

I am sure that had I stayed and Luigi had come to me again I would have believed that it did not touch him, not taint him. Perhaps he was simple rather than Satanic, perhaps a little sophistry would have sufficed, but things had been taken out of my hands and Luigi was out of my bed and my life, my new life next to the old church of Santo Spirito in an apartment that no one had lived in before and where I spent the rest of my nights in Milan.

Mr Corallo

I suppose it had all been planned out by the happy couple. Mrs C had told me at the beginning of our hour that she wanted to help me forget the beautiful young man who had come to rewire my kettle. I had confessed my affair with Luigi but refused to name him and we had spent many hilarious moments when she would suddenly throw an absurd name at me, daring me to own it as my lover's. I do believe she was a little jealous of my making love with another, but she dealt with what has always seemed the basest, albeit the most human, of emotions in the highest of spirits and we would find ourselves breathless with laughing at the dazzling scenarios Mrs C would suggest for the fulfilment of our sex lives in groupings with the entire opposite sex. That she would ever seek to realise them in the flesh was only a fleeting fantasy of my own.

Yet if truth be told, at the very back of my imagination I had always entertained the possibility of such a threesome, and I should have known that Mrs C would always make dreams come true, even if they weren't mine. I was not therefore altogether surprised to find myself in what was theoretically so sordid but in reality so sensual a situation.

We had ended our lesson as usual in Mrs C's bed. My pupil and I were naked and talking when I became aware of another presence – I knew it was not Concetta. I looked over Mrs C's shoulder to see a man leaning against the doorpost with his arms crossed on his wide chest, tall and dark-suited and smiling under a black moustache. It was of course Mr Corallo.

Mrs C followed my eyes and rose to greet him and he wrapped her in his arms and kissed her. Through the discomfort of my shame it was my turn to feel a distinct pang of jealousy, but both pains subsided when Mr C raised his head above her ebony locks and looked straight at me. From his eyes I knew he was still smiling and delighted to see me. My embarrassment should have been far more lasting but I had grown so comfortable in my nudity it seemed the only the appropriate apparel for my time with Mrs C. Concetta's insouciance and Kurt's dogged indifference to all but his own genitals had added to the sense of ease I felt when wandering around the apartment in my skin. The besuited Mr C however, seemed out of place, his sharp dark sleeves around his wife's waist and the soft pale curves of her form emphasised the absurdity of his clothes in this realm of flesh.

Mrs C's back was to me but I realised that she was undoing her husband's Armani tie, unbuttoning his Cerruti shirt and unzipping his trousers – he must have kicked aside his Gucci loafers as I heard them thud against the wall. He shrugged the jacket from his shoulders, his trousers and underpants dropped to the floor. He stepped out of the crumpled circles around his ankles and removed socks as sheer as stockings. Without taking his eyes from my face he grasped his wife's rich buttocks in his wide hands, lifted her up onto his hips and impaled her on his penis. He brought her to the bed and lay her down beside me, still deep inside her. I made to move but Mrs C reached out to clasp my wrist.

"Watch dear Julia, see how his prick moves in and out of me. How thick and magnificent it is."

Mr C raised himself above his wife on tanned and muscular arms. I was transfixed, staring down between their bodies as he pounded into her for several minutes, almost pulling out each time so I could see her swollen lips clinging in vain to his prick, which he eventually fully withdrew.

"Lie back Julia, let us both make love to you."

While her husband stepped back from her spread legs and inserted himself between mine Mrs C pushed me gently back against the pillows then moved down to my cunt, the lips of which she parted with the fingers of one hand while those of the other she wrapped around her husband's prick and drew him into me. Having led him to the right place, he shoved in with an alarming lack of concern, but I was wet enough and his prick was slippery with his wife. For a moment I could feel her fingers between my body and her husband's ringing the base of his penis. As she leant forward to kiss him I looked up to see her magnificent breasts over my face and reached up to touch them. They felt as heavy and full as thighs and I wanted to take them in my mouth which suddenly seemed empty and unused and jealous of the kisses above me. Mrs C understood and poised herself over my face, her cunt over my mouth. It was wet and red and plump and I extended my tongue to lick the little bud standing proud in the soft folds. I knew her tongue was in the mouth of her husband whose prick was so deep in me I felt as if it should burst from my mouth and into her.

I sensed her come above me and the juice flowed down over me, down into my throat and into my hair. She deftly lifted herself from my face and knelt once more beside me, having broken the circle and consequently the spell. Her husband above me was smiling and for only the second time I heard his voice and I wondered whether he had recognised me, the wild and naked bacchante, as the demure, blushing girl who had sped past him in the lobby so long ago.

"She did not wait for us Julia, but I shall wait for you."

Momentarily nonplussed at the bizarreness of the situation I turned to Mrs C who was also smiling at me.

"*Caro mio*, she is used to my tender embraces, don't push so, leave her to me."

He removed himself and lay down next to me. Mrs C put her fingers in my cunt and drew the juice over my clitoris which she rubbed until I came while her husband on the other side leant over and licked the taste of his wife from my face, sliding the flat palms of his hands back and forth over the aching points of my nipples until I lost all sense of my flesh and her flesh and his in the flurry of hands and fingers and mouths and tongues. This was desire at its most basic, stripped of any personality, any perspective, simply flesh on flesh, man and woman so mingled I could not tell them apart, pleasure giving and pleasure taking, a mutual trade in sensation. Yet again Mrs C broke the silence and the spell by suggesting it was her husband's turn to come.

He rolled onto his back and his prick pushed up against the air as if it wanted to fuck the ceiling – one had to admire this man's stamina. We knelt on either side of him and drew our heads together over his erect penis and licked it up and down together, our lips and tongues touching around it, then took it in turns to take it in our mouths. His hands were reaching for our breasts, occasionally catching a nipple, and his breathing grew faster than it had been when exerting himself over our bodies. We both sensed the tightening in his balls and tasted the salty semen in each other's mouths, but to our delight Mr C did not come. He told us both to lay upon the bed – one either side of him – which we did, laughing as we fell back upon the cool pillows. He rolled first onto Mrs C's voluptuous body and inserted his penis between her spread legs and told me, "Come kiss my beautiful wife Julia while I fuck her."

I brought my lips to hers while her husband again pounded away over us. I sensed Mrs C's orgasm rising through her body, her breath quickening in my mouth and felt the now familiar shudder as she came once more. Now her husband was laughing.

"Without me, you came again without me. Maybe Julia will wait for me."

He pulled out of his wife and I lay back and opened my legs for his glistening penis which he inserted with more tenderness this time. Lazy with fulfilment Mrs C's caresses were soft and slow. She slid her long fingers around the stem of hard flesh, between my swollen labia, at one point I felt her fingers inside me with the prick. So wet and wide was I, I could have taken a thousand pricks, a thousand fingers and tongues inside me and still have wanted more – the sensation demanded hyperbole. I thrust my tongue between his lips and felt his breath in time with his push in my cunt, and Mrs C withdrew her hand.

For just one moment we were alone, the two of us, man and woman, aware only of each other, the scene, the situation and Mrs C obliterated in our exclusive need for the body of the other and in that moment I committed the only act of adultery of my life.

Mr C's orgasm rose like a torment through his entire body. I watched as his face grew tight and felt the breath tear his chest apart as it pushed through his clenched teeth in a frantic hiss. When he could hold back no more it burst from his mouth in a bellow of pain and he threw back his head as if someone had plunged a knife between his shoulder blades. So appalled was I at the violence of his coming that I had not felt the rush of semen into me or the slow sad slip of the softening penis. I reached up my arms around his neck and drew him down onto me, stroking his hair, brushing it from his damp forehead, feeling the tears from my own eyes running down into my hair. I was crying, silently at first and then the sobs shook my body and Mr C raised his head in alarm.

"*Cara mia*, what is the matter, did I hurt you?"

I shook my head. In truth I did not know if it was the shock of his brutal orgasm, the lack of my own or the strangeness of my situation. Between two lovers I knew a terrible loneliness and wanted again the feeling of being so at one with the man in my body who did not belong to me. I do not know when Mrs C left the room, but I knew we were now on our own.

Mr C lay on his side and drew me into his arms, rocking me gently back and forth, kissing my tousled head.

"My wife told me you have a great sadness in you, but also a great joy, you must cherish them both."

How many nights had this couple lain in each other's arms and spoken of *cara Giulia*? Mrs C hardly ever spoke of her husband and never mentioned him by name, and I did not ask, knowing perhaps that I would at some point in the proceedings of our love affair have to meet him. But he knew me intimately, had always known me from my very first lesson with Mrs C, and from her first kiss on my amazed mouth he had known every curve of my body, every fold of my skin, the taste and the smell of me and the touch. I was a gift from the adoring wife to the indulgent husband, offered up on the golden platter of this bed.

Mr C's voice drifted back into my head as I grew aware of the hard arms that drew me against his chest.

"Please do not cry *cara*, we never meant to hurt you, we thought it was time, that you would be happy. We were wrong."

He kissed the top of my head resting in the soft, dark fur of his chest and in spite of the brutality of his initial foray into my body I heard a kindness in his voice.

I raised my head to see Mr C's dark eyes gazing down on me. I raised my hand to his smooth cheek then ran my fingers over the roughness of his moustache. I knew we would not be disturbed, Mrs C had given me to her husband and now I was taking him for myself. I brought my mouth to his and felt the dark hairs prickle my lips, tender with too many kisses. His mouth was as rich and soft as my lover's cunt and I licked the fuzzy lips, drawing them between my teeth as I began my languorous assault.

He too was so gentle this time, he stroked me in long sweeps down my arms and along my flanks so that the skin developed a rhythm of its own to beat through my body. Even when his hands moved to my face and brushed through my hair, still damp with my tears, and as his wife had kissed the girl at the water's edge, he kissed the wetness from my cheeks and from my eyelashes and I heard him murmur that I was beautiful.

He moved on top of me and his prick was as rich and smooth as a silk cushion in my cunt, still sore with his previous exertions. He moved slowly over me and in me and I pushed myself against him until I came and the waves of my orgasm flooded out and over his prick. From the lofty heights of my plateau I looked down on this extraordinary man and waited for the fury of his coming to rise, but he smiled and kissed my parted lips and withdrew with all the delicacy of a *maitre d'*.

"I must go now Julia, Concetta will help you to dress. We will meet again."

He stood and walked to the door, then half turned towards me. I think he knew that he looked like a Classical Greek athlete, with the doorposts forming the columns of Apollo's sanctuary. Or was he Zeus and was I one of those young virgins he impregnated in various guises, a master of deception and transformation?

He smiled under his moustache, his wife's enigmatic smile, and he was gone. I lay back on the silky sheets and waited for Concetta to tell me that my bath was run and bring me the sparkling wine that always accompanied my ablutions.

In the pantheon of my gods they were indeed the King and Queen, Zeus and Hera, Jupiter and Juno. And what was I? The worshipful mortal? Or Danae, a receptacle of divine desire? Or the object of desire, truly the beloved?

It seemed to me then that my face and body were the tabula rasa upon which my lovers could project their fantasies, their images of me and of what they wanted me to be. In truth I had lived so long in the skin it had become my natural habitat. Like a glorious baroque mansion, fit for romantic tableaux, I was a backdrop to their divertimenti, not a key player.

But in time I understood. In time I knew, I recognised the adamantine form of the Corallos' relationship – it was a metaphor for my power. When Mr C kissed the tears from my face that day he was not apologising for implicating me in their dreams, for the hurried initiation into troilism and voyeurism, but for overestimating my understanding of the situation, for my not seeing things as they were. Although I could lie between their distinct feminine and masculine forms, they were as one and when

I made love to one I in effect made love to them both. Every word that passed between myself and Mrs C was heard by her husband, every gesture witnessed by him, an admiring audience and eager participant. Perhaps I was wrong in thinking myself the blank canvas of their desire – over the months I had more richly and competently than I could ever have imagined painted myself. Mrs C had been the colours and the textures I had laid upon the canvas as confidently as she had lain me on her bed to kiss and caress. Their exotic penthouse was the setting for my own fantasy of myself.

As I rose from the bath and into the warm towel Concetta wrapped around me I knew myself to be *la bella Venere*. I was and still am Venus rising from the waves of her own desire. I am Venus – the object and the maker of desire, the fantasy and the means to make that fantasy real. I realised then that I could play any role that was required of me, but it would no longer be a reflection of my lover's desire, it would be a projection of my own.

I never made love with them together again. I saw Mr Corallo only once more before I left Milan. In the meantime I continued to see Mrs C and to make love with her but we never mentioned that day, or her husband. She always initiated our lovemaking and our conversation and I realised the subject was closed, in truth I would not have known what to say had she opened it. Jealousy was unjustified but I think it shadowed us anyway. I often thought of myself between them, of them both making love to me; it hurt to think of them making love to each other.

A silent space formed between us. Instead of the joyful complicity of our lovemaking, a cool duplicity on both our parts lent an air of discomfort to the moments without words or deeds. There was no going back. A little more of what I had brought with me to Milan and into the heady air of Mrs C's boudoir was gone. It may have been painted over, but I think it was erased and a deeper, harder piece replaced it.

Street Life

Looking back I was lucky, I was safe. I felt invincible, somehow impregnable. Wandering through the still warm evenings and into the thick nights on my way home from late lessons and later suppers I never felt fear. The darkness that had terrified me all my childhood brought forth no demons in Milan with its wide open spaces full of junkies and whores, its narrow cobbled streets of anonymous tenements and its misty-edged canals lined with beer cellars that circled it like some Dantean Hell. The looks and sounds of the night were lower and lewder than the brazen flatteries of the day but the lechery glanced off my skin like light and the words slithered into the undergrowth of background noise.

I enjoyed the nights in Milan. I delighted in the wicked click of my heels on the flagstones of courtyards and skimming cobblestones in dark smart streets peopled with elegant shadows from the dress shop windows. I grew so bold, or perhaps so arrogant, I even took to walking the whores' streets.

Between Corso Garibaldi and the Castello where the transvestites hung out, there were mazes of piazzas jam-packed with whores' cars. These served as mobile brothels either in the piazza or, if the steamy windows weren't sufficient cover for the more decorous punters, in parking bays off the main ring road – itself a major site for prostitution. One evening Mr Balls crammed Megan and myself into his jade green Porsche and showed us the sights.

The whores were clumped in covens around small fires, either braziers or simply piles of planks probably torn from nearby fences, for effect rather than warmth. Their faces glowed ghastly in the flame-light and as the cars passed they would pull apart their invariably fur coats to reveal naked bodies or lurid flesh bound with leather belts, bras and garters. Leather was actually very much *di moda* – even in the heat a pair of leather trousers was as necessary to an up-to-date wardrobe as the tartan-bowed Yorkshire terriers which the women slipped under their arms like clutch bags.

The whores had their own sort of dogs to deal with – the men who prowled the *autostrada*, sniffing out the hottest bitches. I was stunned at the circus – it was truly obscene – capable of depraving and corrupting the whole of humanity. Sex for sale in its crudest form. Those women who claim that marriage is prostitution have never cruised the outskirts of Milan. Mr Balls was pointing out the prettier ones, usually the transvestites. He appeared to be enjoying himself but Megan kept saying, "It's disgusting, quite disgusting," and eventually, after the third circuit, I asked if we could go home.

We never took the ring road again but I walked the night streets of Milan with an aplomb worthy of professionals, and I wonder to this day if Mr C knew it was his wife's English teacher he approached as I wandered between the whore-strewn cars in Piazza Nera.

"*Ciao cara.*" I felt a hand twist in my loose hair and stopped dead. I did not recognise the voice immediately.

"*Lasciami cazzo, non sono una prostituta.*"

I heard a deep rich laugh behind me and the hand slipped through my hair and on to my shoulder as my assailant drew beside me.

"*Ma cara Giulia, sono io, non ti ricordi di me? Come mai?*"

I turned to see Mr C smiling so broadly his teeth shone under his moustache.

"I'm sorry, I thought you were a stranger."

"Of course you did, how could you know otherwise? I should not have frightened you. But what are you doing here?"

"I'm going home."

"My wife tells me you live near Santo Spirito, you are far away."

Indeed I was, but I told him the night was warm and I wanted to walk, in truth I did not want to return to my apartment. Megan envied me my privacy but a resentful yearning for Luigi amplified in the silence of solitude. When Mr C invited me to have supper with him I was almost relieved at the promise of company, even that of the man whose wife made love to me every week.

I asked him how my student fared and was told she was of course little changed since the previous afternoon when I had seen her. His ironic tone warned me against further mention and I wondered if he wanted to keep our meeting secret from his wife, but surely they had none where I was concerned? I would decide later, but I knew then that I would not have sex with this man ever again. Our business in each other's bodies was finished.

We walked in silence to a nearby restaurant while Mr C lit a cigarette. In the flare of phosphorous his profile looked uncomfortably cruel. He screwed up his eyes against the acrid smoke and I realised he was probably much older than his wife. I recalled the athletic firmness of his body and the determined energy of his prick but when we fucked I had not really seen him.

I had plenty of time to observe him now and as we sat opposite each other, the food and wine between us, I learnt the lines of his face, the eyes that disappeared into delighted creases every time he laughed, the force of his jaw and the deep red lips under his still dark moustache. He was certainly a handsome man, but his attraction lay not so much in his features but as his unashamed masculinity. For all his elegant clothes, his impeccable manners at table and his easy after dinner conversation, the man was just that – the unadulterated male. As such he was the perfect complement to his wife in whom was apotheosised the female of the species, all curves and roundness and generous flesh, soft hair, soft eyes, and breasts La Cicciolina would have died for. You were always aware of the magnificent body under her clothes, just as I knew Mr C's erection was a permanent fixture.

It was between us now and a part of us, the most basic of responses and yet the most hallowed – like some primal magic, the penis erect between and before all of us, our undoing and our making. It rent the veil of our inhibitions and consumed our social pretences in a bonfire of vanities. There was no disguising its intent. The mystery lay in its genesis, that this marvellous piece of flesh could rise for me and the stapled crease of a centrefold, for the touch of my skin or the shudder of rubber; was I to be flattered or insulted? Before me I saw homo erectus, albeit clad in Gianfranco Ferré, his desire striding the earth in search of not me in particular, but woman.

Walking the streets of Milan that night had I been seeking man, that erect penis, that anonymous column, the naked, unmitigated sex thing? I had had everything else.

By way of an opening into a heavy silence between Mr C's postprandial cigarette and my distraction I asked him if he had ever been with a prostitute.

"Of course, with many."

"When?"

"Then, now, but mostly when I was younger, before I was married."

"But you still do, now?"

"I told you. Why shouldn't I now?"

"Because you are married."

"Really *cara*, I don't believe you think that makes any difference, do you? Sex is an appetite, a taste. I am eating in this particular restaurant because tonight I wanted this particular food, tomorrow I will eat elsewhere, I may even eat at home with my wife, that is if she isn't eating out herself or having an English lesson."

I think I almost blushed. I apologised for asking so personal and impertinent a question, but Mr C smiled: "No, *cara*, you know what I am talking about. You think that sex, that what we did, must be so intimate and yet you apologise for asking me a personal question. You understand that you do not know any more about me now than before we fucked. Yes, you know how my body feels when it is on you, how my prick feels inside you and how I come. You do not know how I think, how I feel, how I love, how I hate. But what you know is enough."

Yes, I knew what pleasure there is to be had in surfaces, the stunning logic of interlocking forms. Prick in cunt, yin and yang, male and female, first principles, the basics.

"I go to prostitutes because I like anonymous sex, literally sex without names, without personality. I do not want to know the woman. I never have sex with the same woman twice, in that way I practise a sort of monogamy. I do not want to get inside her head, I want to be inside her body. Such sex is the ultimate liberation for me, unfettered by expectation, by significance, the purest of pleasures, the original sin."

"Is it important to pay for it?"

"Of course. It makes it clean, without misunderstanding."

"A power thing, you paying the woman, you being the one in control, the one who demands?"

"Again Julia, you know what I mean but you would rather you did not. All sex is power. Ah, you say, of course it is because knowledge is power and what better way to know someone than to fuck her, as if sex were the secret to our souls. The only knowledge we acquire in sex is about ourselves. If it is about control it is again of the self, knowing how far we can go, when to stop, if ever to stop. But I digress. Yes, sex is about power, power play.

"As for being the one who demands – it does not begin with me, but with you. When I fuck you I acknowledge your power to excite my desire and in wanting me to fuck you, you acknowledge your power to fulfil that desire. I am a tool of your sexuality fashioned by your needs, by desire itself.

"In fact *cara*, I am sure there have been occasions when you didn't really want a man, had never considered him as a possible lover, but his desire was strong enough for both of you because there is nothing so seductive to a woman as a man hell bent on seducing her. It was not the man who aroused you, it was his lust for you – you saw yourself as he saw you, tasted your power over him and paradoxically succumbed to it, to yourself. In effect you could have sex with any man, as long as he wanted you so very much – you could even enjoy it."

I disagreed, was I to blame for the effect of my sex on the random phallus, and therefore honour bound to service it? I think not. But the balance of power between seducer and seduced? I remembered Mr P's unprepossessing form, the drenched knickers that I left between the pages of his textbook and I shifted uncomfortably in my chair.

"But what of the prostitute? Where does she fit in?"

Mr C lit another cigarette with his ultra-slim silver lighter and pushed his own chair slightly back from the table to cross his legs with more ease.

"I do find it curious that the prostitute is so pitied and despised. Surely she is an icon of women's power over men – she can lower her lashes, lift her skirt and we are instantly lost. Our blood drains from our brains and empties out every logical thought. All we can see is her mouth and our pricks in it, all we can smell is her cunt. If we have any control over her it is financial, but remember, even there if we do not pay we do not get."

"But you can always get it – you can take it by force if it isn't given for money."

"You talk of rape, I talk of sex – of course there is a connection in that the penis is used in both instances, in the one as a weapon, in the other as an instrument of pleasure. But rape is not sex, nothing to do with desire. Rape is about psychological and psychical deformity – it is not about power, it is about weakness, the weakness of a man afraid."

I thought of the women on the ring road. I recalled the cars and their occupants running on testosterone, heard again the verbal abuse these disempowered creatures perpetrated on the whores. I knew my host merely had a perspective not the whole picture, but I preferred his view to mine, and it suited my purpose to stay ahead. I did not contradict him again.

He continued, "I know you think it sordid but in fact the whole transaction is so very clean – sex between prostitute and client is the only honest sex, it is sex for its own sake. It accepts the nature of desire, defines it. The act is self-contained, an end in itself. In real life sex refuses to recognise its boundaries, demands to be taken seriously, to be significant. If it is good we want it again and habit soon rears its dreary head. If we knew that once was enough, either because it could not possibly be bettered and the spell could not be cast again, or because it was so disappointing, we seek to justify the act, we need an excuse. We insist on the guilt if it was nothing more than pleasure, the regret if it was anything less. We believe, wrongly, that sex must be part of something bigger, some plan, some future. I would say forget the future and the past – in sex we can do that, we can lose ourselves – just enjoy the moment."

Yes, again, I did understand. Between the skin of this man and his wife I had known the oblivion of self, but how much of that feeling was due to knowing not only their names but the setting, the safety, the trust that hours in their home and company had induced? Mr C was speaking of sex, not with lovers who made love with affection and memory and words, but with strangers, with nameless bodies. I had never known sex like that and I wanted to but I was not prepared to join the prostitutes in the square or take my chances on the dark backseats of the ring road punters. There must be another way and this man knew it.

"But the moment must end, what then?"

"You kiss it goodbye, and wait for the next one."

"And while you are waiting for the next anonymous fuck you make habitual love to the named one who loves you, the one who knows your name, and is there no guilt in all this?"

I had moved unbidden from the abstract to the particular, to the personal, and his wife was suddenly so vivid in my mind's eye that Mr C saw her too.

"I told you, we have an understanding. No, there is

no guilt because there is no need for such crass self-indulgence. I do nothing for which I might feel guilt since that is a sure indication it is the wrong thing to do. I take it you are speaking of infidelity. I am faithful in my own way."

In my own way – the hubris of this man was utterly seductive. I let myself succumb to his sophistry, I would deal with my own truths at another time. For now I entered into the thrall of my host. Whether he was also to be my pimp or procurer was for me to decide.

"Enough talking, *cara*. Let us take a walk. We will have champagne at my club, I think you are ready for it."

The night, even at this late hour, was full of people, many of them pooled under the white light of the wide apart street lamps – people out to eat, to be entertained, to buy drugs or sex or both, or to window shop in the occasional out of the centre emporium. We walked slowly, talking little, Mr C drawing on his sharp cigarette. Then suddenly he flung it in the gutter and took my arm to lead me down a narrow alley to the canal. He was now silent and his pace increased, he almost pulled me along the water's edge and over a humpback bridge and down another alley to a small dark doorway in an otherwise blank brick wall. He knocked on the door and it was opened immediately by a broad man in an evening suit who greeted Mr C and stood to one side so we could go past him into the long dim corridor.

I drew back in an attempt to extricate my wrist from his grasp but he only tightened the bracelet of his perfectly manicured fingers.

"*Ma Giulia, come mai?*" He was smiling but not with amusement. I was aware of an upward shift of the bouncer's eyebrows and a transference of power between the two men – my hesitation had compromised Mr C. He released my wrist and, still smiling, shrugged his shoulders.

"I was wrong – there is always a first time I suppose."

I could do no more than stammer an apology, bewildered, stymied even by my sudden anxiety.

"Run home *Giulia*, run to mamma."

He turned on his unworn heels and stepped sharply down the corridor and I was ushered back through the door which was shut thickly behind me.

In a strange place in so many ways, my nocturnal meanderings had drawn a thread across the labyrinthine city and I was soon back on more familiar ground. It took some time longer to reach Santo Spirito and much longer to deal with the sense of having failed. I had thought myself braver, but it would appear my spirit was not as free as Mr C had assumed, my mind not as broad or as curious – no daughter of Eve me. As the hour of my next lesson with Mrs C approached my sense of self-esteem retreated.

Berry Red

I cancelled our next lesson, feigning heatstroke, which was certainly a possible affliction at the time. The Summer had seemed endless, day after day of fulsome heat and brilliance augmenting in the empty squares and parks where only the tourists and myself wandered, unaware that Milan was in exodus. The other teachers had taken an apartment in Lerici for a couple of weeks. Although tempted by its romantic associations with my favourite poet, whose drowned body had been washed up on its shore, I decided to enjoy a city that grew more majestic in its solitude. A few of my students had remained and I went from house to house visiting and taking cake and wine and slipping ever more easily into Italian ways. Until, ashamed at my cowardice, I girded my trembling and by now lonely loins and called Mrs C to say I was recovered and did she desire a lesson?

"One last one," she said, before even Mrs C was to desert Milan and me.

I arrived that afternoon to find the lamé bedspread covered in Michelin maps.

"You are pale *cara*, perhaps your head still pains you?" She bestowed a soft kiss on my forehead and the genuine concern never left her eyes, which I hardly dared meet, as she continued. "You should get out of the city for a few days, I don't like to think of you here on your own. We have to go down South to see my family – not for long, but they expect it of me."

A slight pain in my chest, an ache along the sternum. "We" ... him. Had he told her how I had shamed him? Had she been there, in that place, waiting for both of us? And then harder than the shame, the unknowing, was the sense of my outsiderness, not just from her marriage but her life. Even more than the thought of my lover with her husband, I resented her family. What were they like? What mother had raised this strange and lovely woman at my side? What did she think of her son-in-law? Her daughter had certainly made a good, if unorthodox, match. So many questions, other connections, and my lover in a context so far from that in which we conducted our relationship.

Mrs C took my hand but lowered her head over the maps. "Would you travel alone?"

Of course I would and had, often taking the train to Como for Sunday lunch. In fact I had seen much of Lombardy since my arrival in its capital. I reminded Mrs C of the weekend Megan and I had been as far as Bologna with its listing towers then on to Ferrara with its fairytale castle; of another time Mr Balls had driven us to Verona for a concert in the Coliseum and supper in the strange elliptical piazza. I had stood beneath Juliet's balcony in the house of the Capuleti, distressed at the graffiti that defaced the walls inside and out, and photographed our own star-crossed lovers, Megan and Mr Balls, standing either side of a rather fey bronze statue of the tragic heroine.

"But this is not really travelling *Giulia*. I wish I could take you to Calabria but at the least you should see Tuscany. We have an apartment in Florence, overlooking the Arno. My husband has a wonderful library there. I know how you love books."

She paused and smiled broadly.

"Not that you will have any time to read, what with everything to see in Florence. You can drive down to Genova and along the coast and then return over the mountains. There you will certainly find fresh air. Alia is lovely, I know of a good *pensione*. Yes, you must go."

Suddenly, alone in Milan without lovers or friends did not seem so very appealing.

"How long will it take me by train?"

"Ah, you cannot go by train, it is too complicated, too slow. You can drive, can you not?"

I had taken my test the week after my seventeenth birthday and much to everyone's amazement, had passed. My friends considered me an 'ambitious' driver – I simply drove too fast. Mrs C dismissed my lack of experience and offered me her 'city' car, her berry red Fiat Cinque Cento.

What the car lacked in comfort it made up for in an infra dig style and, young and cocksure, I believed Mrs C when she assured me it was as easy as pushing a shopping trolley (the which I was sure she had never done).

"I will arrange the insurance if that will make you feel better – you English are so, how do you say? Law-abiding. Come again tomorrow and you can drive us to Bergamo, the exercise will do you good. I am meeting a friend there, he will be glad to entertain us both."

I trusted there was no sexual innuendo in her choice of words – I would not be offered up again for the delectation of Mrs C's men. In the event, he was an elderly acquaintance who wined and dined us in a beautiful restaurant in the old town on top of a steep hill. Mrs C said I was in training for the mountains.

Megan called from the seaside to persuade me to join them: "It's glorious here Jools, but I'm missing you, the others are so boring." The heat and alcohol rendered her companions comatose. She assured me that Jack would not be a problem, having taken off to San Remo in the convertible Porsche of what Megan sniffily deemed to be a "very well preserved woman." His return was not imminent.

She was rather put out when I told her of my intended journey to the Corallos' apartment. She thought the whole venture most improper, suggesting that my friends wanted more from me than English lessons for free. I assured her there was nothing more I could give them.

I juddered along from Milan to Genova and turned right along the coast. The sea between the darkness of the tunnels cut into the rockface was dazzling and the on-off effect of the light made me dizzy, as did the height. The road was built on stilts that carried it from one mountain to another over the towns of the Italian Riviera: Rapallo, La Spezia, Viareggio and my compatriots sunning themselves hundreds of feet below it. At Livorno I turned left to Florence.

Artists and Models

At that point in my life I had not visited many cities but Florence to me seemed the most magical place on my small earth. Even now, when I pull up in the Piazza di Michelangelo my pulse is racing with pleasure at the beauty of the city laid out below. In the early evening the Arno flows through it like a ribbon of pink and the dome of the cathedral glows rose and the soft stone turns the colour of skin. My passion for the place is as physical as if it had fucked me, as if I had run my fingers over every surface.

I entered Florence for the first time through Porta Romana and, having driven up and down the wrong streets the wrong way and across the river twice, I finally pulled up beside a police car, the occupants of which were so obviously taken with the contents of the Fiat that I risked communication and asked them to direct me to Mr C's apartment. They told me to follow them and within minutes I was at the correct address.

Exhausted by the journey, I did not pay much attention to the architecture and handed myself over to the porter who took my bag and the car keys, informed me that the building was too old to accommodate a lift and bade me follow him up the marble staircase. It curved up and up and every step seemed deeper and wider. I hadn't the breath to curse my elevated friends but again the Corallos had taken a space as close to the clouds as possible and again they had the entire top floor.

The porter opened the massive wooden door into a huge panelled room, the lamps lit and the curtains drawn against the evening. He told me that the maid would come every day to clean the apartment and ensure there was food in the fridge and, if I so desired, she would prepare hot meals. I assured him this would not be necessary, I would eat out. I never met the maid, like Beauty in the Beast's castle I was waited on by invisible hands which turned down my sheets and laid out my nightdress, made the bed in the morning and put fresh flowers in the lounge every day.

As the door closed behind the porter my lassitude vanished and I tore through the place like a curious child. Most of the rooms were locked. Only my bedroom, a luxurious but – in view of Mrs C's tendency to overkill – tasteful boudoir with antique furniture and pale brocade, the opulent bathroom, kitchen and lounge were accessible.

The lounge was as old-fashioned as the Milan apartment's was modern – dark wood and glass-fronted bookcases and a huge Chinese carpet under the leather-studded suite. The ornaments were obviously valuable: cloisonné, Lalique, and all the lamps were Le Gallé, not a Sailor angelpoise in sight. Much to my disappointment the bookcases were locked but I found the key in a small silver dish on the night table next to the bed. It was curly and gold and could only have fitted those locks. It was certainly fitting that it should be kept in the boudoir. Every single one of the volumes was filled with descriptions and depictions of lovemaking and sex.

They were arranged historically and alphabetically from Boccacio to Bataille, De Sade to Sacher-Masoch, Rabelais to Réage, names and titles I did not know then but with which over those few nights I became closely acquainted. Every culture was represented in the collection – pillow books from China and Japan stuffed with huge genitalia, the Perfumed Gardens of the East and the *Kama Sutra*, and Western tales of sexual awakenings and corruption.

Many of the books were in French. The finest was bound in white leather with gold lettering and illustrated with exquisite watercolour plates by a surrealist artist, Leonor Fini. It began with the journey of a beautiful young woman to a Chateau where her future as O awaits. Her lover blindfolds her and bids her remove her underwear. She spends the rest of the book knickerless and powerless as the tale turns into a litany of ritual torture and mutilation that the woman professes to enjoy. I was not convinced even then.

The book was well-written, moving in part, disturbing but not delighting and I discarded it in favour of other tomes, some from the seventeenth century with browning pages and the mustiness of age, others with glossy garish covers and a whole row of green paperbacks from the fifties.

I selected a few titles from the shelves and, a bottle of Chianti uncorked beside me, I settled into the sofa to read. The pleasures of Florence would wait until tomorrow, that night the books were my bedfellows. The words aroused and seduced me and I turned the pages with the indecent hurry of disrobing a lover. The images filled my head as the phrases became palpable and I indulged in the most hedonistic voyeurism, inconceivable to me before I experienced it on the page. My fingers slid down the page and under my skirt, under my knickers and into my naked cunt. But they were not my fingers, they were the fingers of all the lovers in all the minds of all the writers of these fictions – *Galeotto fu il libro e chi lo scrisse*.

The words blurred and in the distraction of my orgasm I dropped the book, but my blood was up, I had sex in the head and I reached for another and another orgasm, and again until I could see no more and my fingers were too wet to turn the page and the leather of the sofa was slippery with my come. I pushed all the books, preciously rare and accessibly popular, onto the floor and fell to sleep, exhausted and sated and probably drunk.

I awoke hours later with a fierce thirst and a sense of relief; I imagined my shame had the maid found me in the midst of this literary decadence. I replaced the books in the cabinets and the key in the silver dish and lay upon the bed to sleep out the dawn.

The sun finally pushed its way through the curtains and under my heavy eyelids. Hunger dragged my reluctant form to the kitchen. The maid had been and laid out fruit and brioche for my breakfast, there was even a teapot and Earl Grey tea; my friends had thought of everything. The kitchen windows were open and I looked out over the celestial city and suddenly the time was too short, the whole of Florence, with its galleries, its gardens and shops, was waiting.

I left the Fiat in the garage and wandered *a piedi* and utterly entranced down the narrow streets and into the huge piazzas. I walked across the Ponte Vecchio glittering with goldsmiths, down Via Tornabuoni lined with the most stylish shops in the sophisticated world, around the Pitti Palace and the Piazza della Signora with its great green Neptune and nymphs cooling themselves in the fountain. I entered with reverence the Farmacia di Santa Maria Novella, established four hundred years ago by the Dominican friars, to collect an order of toiletries for Mrs C. I purchased a bottle of Catherine de Medici's Acqua di Cologna and a small red box of Carta di Armenia – slips of paper one burnt to release the incense with which they were impregnated.

My point of pilgrimage was however, the Uffizi, and I went to pay homage in the room where Botticelli's paintings hung. Every time I wonder if the delight will dull, if somehow the image printed on my retina by such constant exposure to its replicated form will eventually supersede the reality. But no, all the posters and postcards and pizza menus of the past few decades have not been able to diminish my joy on beholding the real Venus at her birth.

I fell in love with Simonetta Vespucci as profoundly as had poor Sandro. I loved her in all her incarnations, as Pallas, as Flora and Voluptas, as the Madonna adored by angels and Magi, but I loved her best as Venus, *la mia bella Venere*. I stood before the canvas and resented the glass that lay between her skin and my outstretched hand.

"*Signorina, non si toccano i quadri. Ma comprendo la sua tentazione.*"

I drew back my hand, alarmed that the attendant, however understanding, would ask me to leave. Yet the forty-something man that stood beside me had neither the air nor the apparel of a gallery guard. He was dressed in jeans and a loose white shirt, and a neat greying beard and moustache graced a grand face. He had authority, even if not on the gallery's behalf, and I felt the need to apologise. I did so in English, hoping that a tourist would be more readily forgiven.

"My dear Miss, I was only trying to warn you, all the canvasses are wired. But I do understand, I would like to touch her too. The skin is so perfect, so pale, like the inside of a shell. I believe the word is nacreous, no?"

I nodded, constantly ashamed at the eloquence of others in my own language, constantly charmed by the sound of it in Italian mouths.

"The hair is so soft, and the light in it, indescribable, no? But I have been watching you and your hair, it is the same colour and your skin, it is so pale and your mouth, as sweet as Simonetta's."

I smiled, flattered at the novelty of his approach. It was of course the hair, the hair with which I could have bound Mr Parola, the hair in which Mr C had twisted his fingers, the hair his wife brushed with tenderness down over my naked shoulders murmuring, "You are my Venus, *cara*. Botticelli imagined you – I have *la realtá* here with me."

"I am sorry, I have disturbed you. Please do not think me, how do you say? Forward. I am an artist and I was looking at you only as an artist looks at a beautiful woman, as a woman he would like to paint."

I never entirely lost the trusting, gullible side of my nature and he did look rather like my idea of an artist. He introduced himself as Guido, a lover of women, wine and the Italian Renaissance, its art, architecture and philosophies. He told me about the Neoplatonists who had inspired and directed the course of Botticelli's work and of the myths on which they had based their philosophies of the One and the Many. In lowered tones he told me of Dionysian revels where the god is torn to pieces, sacrificed to mutation; of the castration of Uranus and his dismembered genitals dispersing semen on the waters as the foam, the aphros, from which Venus his daughter is born. He told me how she is blown by the winds of passion to the shores of Cyprus where the hour of Spring awaits her with a mantle for her modesty.

He asked why I was fascinated by this particular painting. I really couldn't say beyond knowing it to be one of the loveliest images I had ever beheld.

"I would say it is because you and Venus are kindred spirits, naive yet knowing, chaste yet sensuous. That is how you appear to me. Plato explained the dual nature of the goddess of love by giving her two names, two forms, Aphrodite Pandemos and Aphrodite Urania. Pandemos means of all the people, Urania – of the sky. You see Venus is both the woman we have in our bed to satisfy our lust and hers and the goddess who is unattainable, our fantasy of love, the ideal we can never achieve."

I had never been compared to a philosophy before. Was this man a hopeful lover of wisdom or myself? In the gap of my unvoiced questions he continued, "You are like her, approachable but so distant. You know you can trust me, but you seem suspicious. Do not be. I know what I say must sound strange but I want only one thing, presumptuous though it may be to ask anything of you, I want only your time."

Before I had time to consider his request – or was it his offer? – a voice cut through the hot quiet air.

"*Professore, sempre qui, sempre questi quadri metafisici. La Rinascente, i Medici, i Papi, gli uomini, mi fanno schifo e lei non può cambiare le mie convinzioni.*"

Guido smiled indugently at the young virago, loud and vibrant as her voice, striding across the gallery towards us.

"Isabella, how good to see you, though I am sure you are not here to work. Some romantic friend's idea of a suitable meeting place perhaps? This is...", and here he paused, both of us suddenly aware that we had been conversing for a considerable length of time and he knew nothing about me, not even my name.

"Julia."

He cast his smile over me and said, "Julia, ah, a suitable name, it means soft-haired."

Isabella extended her silver-ringed hand across Guido's admiring musings, "Forgive me interrupting, I am a student at the academy of Fine Art, Guido is my teacher and a very great artist, but he has a problem – he is also a philosopher and he insists all these canvasses are treatises on obscure Renaissance thought. I think they are merely bedroom decoration for a bunch of dirty old men who had to dress up their centrefolds in classical allusion."

At this Guido raised his hands to his head and shook his grizzled mane in mock horror, "Isabella, you only say these things to annoy me, I know you understand really."

Isabella, if subject to a healthy disregard for solemnity, did of course know the value of perfection and relented, "OK, they are lovely, and Plotinus and Ficino may have put a few ideas in Sandro's head. But philosphy? No. Just lust, just another way of fucking his model. Of course it has been said that sex is art. Poor Simonetta, mistress of a de Medici, fabled for her beauty, dead at twenty-three from consumption. You know, Julia, you look a bit like her? I keep telling the Professor however, that he is far too handsome to play Botticelli. Do you know what Botticelli means Julia? It means the little barrel."

She paused to draw breath and to pat her professor's non-existent beer belly and I was instantly rather piqued by this show of familiarity, unusual between pupil and student (Mr Parola and Mrs C were exceptions to the rule) in a country that took its education very seriously.

"Well, I must go, I'm late. I'm meeting Giovanni in La Tribuna, he is doing a copy of Carolina di Pontormo, miserable bitch. That is right is it not, bitch?"

She didn't wait for a reply and was gone in a rush of musk into the long statue-lined corridor, leaving me to wonder if she had heard our conversation about the painting and consequently, her tutor's request to paint me.

"Isabella is impossible, but she will be a good designer one day. She comes here to study the fabrics and the patterns in these paintings, perhaps the skin does not interest her so much. You see I am alone in my passion for Botticelli, although even Isabella understood why I should paint you."

So that really was what he wanted of me – I was flattered, even if a little miffed at so innocent a request. I could certainly spend the rest of the afternoon with him but explained my stay in Florence was brief.

"I will be content with a few sketches. I have a studio just outside the city walls, we can be there in twenty minutes."

I affected the air of one who is a constant muse and said of course he could draw me, but why not here, why not down by the river which flowed past the Uffizi and along which you could always see amateurs and artists painting the timeless view of the Ponte Vecchio?

"Because I do not have my materials, because the setting would not be right. Besides I would like you to see my house, I think it is a special place, in the hills above Florence, You can see the whole city from my balcony."

I agreed and we hurried through the gallery, Guido pointing out his favourite pieces and pausing only in the jewel-like Tribuna. Isabelle and Giovanni were not there but I beheld the incandescent face of Carolina di Pontormo who seemed haughty rather than miserable, and the lovely Medici *Venus* whose pose Botticelli had borrowed for his own.

Reminding me that I was a tourist, Guido enticed me into a horse-drawn trap and we clopped our slow way through the traffic and narrow streets out of Porta San Miniato and up Via di Belvedere. We passed the Fort and stopped at the Piazza di Michelangelo where I rushed from wall to wall to take in the stunning view and catch my breath, speechless with wonder.

I could have stayed for hours. Between the curios of the Algerian traders spread upon the ground and the glorious vistas of Florence all around there was much to amuse me, but Guido insisted the light would fail if we did not hurry. The poor horse was flicked to a canter up a steep path and into a grove of cypress trees.

Guido's house was itself a work of art. The interior was a veritable gallery of masterpieces: he was a collector as well as a provider. The studio was high and huge and full of white light filtering through the opaque glass of the ceiling. There were small stools on which were balanced palettes covered in multi-coloured wormcasts scattered between several easels, all bearing canvasses of different images at different stages of completion. One was of a nude leaning against a pillar. I knew then how Guido wanted to draw me and I was not shy or afraid. It was how I had always wanted to be created. My breath grew short and I wondered if it was due to the linseed oil and turpentine or an intimation of arousal at the thought of my own nakedness. I asked Guido if he might open a window and he lifted a lever that opened the roof. I was instantly showered in golden afternoon light and I revelled in its warmth and the artist's admiration.

"Now my dear girl, I would like you to walk around, to relax, and when you feel comfortable I would like you to undress."

"You wish to draw me nude?"

I knew but I wanted him to say it.

"How else? You are shy?"

"No, not shy. I just need a little time."

"As you please. I will bring us some fruit and cheese and wine."

He left the room and I walked through the unctuous air, lifting the coloured cloths that lay upon chairs and small tables, uncovering jars and vases and bowls of the kind of ceramic particular to Florence, all props perhaps.

I removed my sandals and felt the wooden floor smooth with dust and warm under my feet. I unzipped my dress and unhooked my bra, pulling it through the armholes as I had seen Jill do on the train from school when she was meeting a lover at the other end. I removed my knickers and pushed both them and the bra into my shoulder bag already brimful with trinkets from the market around the Medici Chapel. I left my dress undone but on my body.

I was surprised, annoyed even, at the renaissance of my modesty. I had been naked before many men. I had sat in a state of total *déshabillement* before Mr P, but in all these circumstances my nudity was a means to an end, to sex, with men, women or myself and the eyes that fell upon me would soon be joined by curious or familiar hands. But this relentless scrutiny, how would it feel?

As if to lead me from my anxiety Guido called out, "Come and eat, drink some wine. I will begin sketching as you move around. Feel free to sit or stand as you please."

I took some grapes and a short thick glass of cold white wine from an unlabelled flask and settled into a pile of cushions. Guido was seated on a low stool in front of an easel, from the scratching sounds I realised he was using charcoal. His hand moved fast across the paper and my curiosity got the better of me so I rose and walked round to see what he had drawn.

The shock of recognition was breathtaking – it was me. My head, my hair, the long curve of my arms and my feet tucked up, just visible under my skirt. He had drawn my neck and my décolletage, the shadow of my breasts in the folds of my dress and I knew it was foolish and there was no need for shame, he could only guess at the reality and the reality was far grander. I walked back into the centre of the room and lifted the straps off my shoulders and let the dress fall to the floor.

I looked at Guido who was looking at me, at all of me, "*Davvero, la mia Venere.* And a natural blonde."

He laughed, and any tension dissipated before the sound of his amusement had stilled in the air.

"In fact you are so fair you seem even more naked, as naked as every great Venus, Titian's, Tintoretto's and Giorgione's. But you are still my Venus, with golden hair and a body of pearl and I will paint you as such. Will you pose for me? Will you let me arrange you?"

I nodded my assent, too shy yet elated to speak and feeling like an armful of flowers. I stood still as a statue while he tied a swathe of gold-coloured silk to my hair at the nape of my neck and draped it down over my left shoulder to create the effect of Simonetta's ankle-length tresses. He told me to take the end in my hand and place it between my legs.

My desire made me bold, "Show me how."

And he took the silk and placed it over my cunt. I could feel the heat of his hands through the fabric and I wanted him to touch me there, touch me inside where I was wet. He told me to put my hand on his. I covered it with my fingers and pushed him against me and for a brief moment I knew his fingers slipped with the silk between the lips of my cunt and Guido knew I wanted him and I felt his breath grow short over my shoulder.

"Now I will remove my hand but keep yours there, just below, just between your thighs."

My disappointment was audible but Guido took my other arm and bent it across my chest, to cover one breast and rest above the other. My nipples were hard and he could not have failed to see their forceful rise, but he ran his hands down my right leg to the knee which he coaxed forward until only the toes of that foot were touching the ground. He pulled one of the cushions under my raised foot and told me to rest on it when the pose became uncomfortable. As he stood I felt his breath rising on my body like a hot wind and when he was fully upright, a little taller than me, I felt it again in my hair ruffling the loose strands. I looked up and he took my face in his two gentle palms and tilted my head to the right.

In his dark brown eyes I saw myself reflected, another image of myself, another fantasy. I smiled but Guido was stern: "No, you must not smile. I would rather you looked sad than happy, but it's not sad really, it's nostalgic I think?"

His face was so close I could have kissed him but I parted my lips to suggest he meant 'wistful'.

He withdrew his hands and with what was probably a characteristically quizzical air said, "Wistful? This sounds a beautiful word, like blowing a kiss. Yes, be wistful."

He walked back to the easel, tore the charcoaled paper from the board and replaced it with another larger and thicker sheet the colour of ivory. He drew up a table covered in tiny tubes of paint which he squeezed into various small china dishes.

Without lifting his eyes from the table he explained, "My preferred medium is oils but I will use watercolour. These will dry quickly enough to do several sketches. The lead of a pencil cannot express the delicate rose of your skin or the light in your hair."

I am sure I must have preened.

He dipped a brush in one of the many jars half full of water and turned to the easel and me. He was seated once more because, he explained, he wanted to look up at me. I wondered if this were visually to elongate my limbs which could never stretch to those of Botticelli's nude, save perhaps under the influence of Mr C's champagne.

I had been so absorbed in the preparations of the artist I had forgotten myself but when the activity ceased and the only sound in the room was my heartbeat I knew again my nudity. The brush was poised in the air while Guido's eyes flew over me, seeking the point of commencement. I held my breath as I waited for the brush to fall, as if it were the man's fingertip above my raised nipple. His decision made, his movements across the paper were smooth and fast and then he would pause and look again. His gaze was as arousing as Luigi's tongue, as sensuous as Mrs C's fingers stroking down my neck around my breasts across my belly and into the very heart of me. Guido knew the inside of my head well as my external form but he did not stir from his stool.

Whether I grew uncomfortable from the position or the constant rush and dissipation of sensation to the surface of my skin was irrelevant to the artist, it was merely noted and he suggested I walk around for a few moments and refresh myself. I was hot under the light, albeit of the low soft afternoon sun, and my skin was shiny with sweat.

I took a cloth to wipe myself down but Guido cried out, "No, no, please do not dry yourself. The moisture, it heightens the shadows and highlights your curves. And the heat, it makes you even more pink, I think you would say 'flushed', in Italian we say *arrossito* – to become red like a rose."

I shrugged my sore shoulders and my retort was rather petulant, "The breath of those zephyrs would be rather welcome."

I seemed to be not so much a sex object as an *objet d'art*, some insensate matter to be manipulated and moulded by the hand of a self-styled creator. I wanted to be this man's inspiration, not his still-life. And I was so tired with standing still.

Guido was following me around the room with his eyes, his hand never still on the paper.

"Julia, I am sorry. Sometimes I forget I am selfish because I am running against the sun. I could light candles but the effect would not be right. I will not be much longer and then you can shower and we will go and eat. I will take you to San Gimignano. We must be there before dark."

I took up my pose once again. Guido did not arrange me this time and before my limbs grew weary he put down his brush and announced, "*Abbiamo finito.*"

He came up to me and untied the gold from my hair and lowered my arms. He stood before me and once more took my head in his hands and turned it towards him. I winced as the tendons stretched and relaxed, having been pulled and compressed into the wistful angle. He slid his hands to my neck and began gently rubbing it, his thumbs running up and down my throat, his fingers pressing along my twisted vertebrae.

"*Povera Venere, bella Venere*, now Venus must bathe and the warm water will relax her."

He dropped his hands to my shoulders and I thought he would kiss me, and he did, on my forehead. I sighed and he led me out of the studio into a large stark room with only a bed covered in a white sheet and one huge canvas on the wall behind it. Guido followed my eyes, "My wife, she was very beautiful."

The woman's long white back was towards me and her head was turned over her shoulder, presenting a profile of linear perfection. Her dark hair was caught up with an elaborate pin revealing the lobe of her ear from which hung a pearl, the only other ornament on her body. She seemed to float in the pale blue of the background, her frame was fine and sinuous and spare, ethereal.

I felt suddenly plump.

"Where is she now?"

"Dead. I live here on my own. Come, through here," and he led me into a much smaller, but similarly monastic room with only a shower cubicle and washbasin, the hermit's cell in a cinquecento cathedral.

"Be careful, the water is hot and forceful. I will bring you a towel and your things."

The floor of the shower was ridged like a scallop shell and the soap released a smell of the sea as I rubbed it over my body, the water beating down on me like hard rain. I lifted my face and felt the water through my hair and in my eyes and nose and mouth and when I had nearly drowned I found the shore of consciousness and the bathroom floor, born again. It took both hands to turn the tide of the water and the rush had been so loud I had not heard Guido enter.

On a wooden stool I found a towel and my bag crumpled with my clothes. These seemed too shabby now to put against my much admired skin. Guido had obviously thought so as well and I heard his voice from the bedroom, "Julia, I have left something you might prefer to wear on the bed. I keep some clothes for the models. I will wait for you on the balcony."

How strange that we had grown shy of each other. The dress lay like a shadow on the white cover, dove grey and as long and finely pleated as a Fortuny. It smelt of roses, and whether it had come from his wife's wardrobe or a prop cupboard its essential exquisiteness rendered it a covetous thing. I drew it over my damp naked body with a gasp of excitement. There was a pair of silver sandals with silver thongs to tie around my ankles and a silver braid for my hair. I was grateful for Guido's consistency; I would be a goddess until we parted. I was not sure if the look was *di moda* for *a trattoria* in San Gimignano, but as an artist's muse I was suited for my purpose.

Guido's car was old and wide, unlike the bright new toy in which I had recently traversed Tuscany, but it took us from Florence to the city of the fair towers before the sun went down and I beheld the magical hill of San Gimignano in the rose glow of a Tuscan twilight. Like a strange Greek temple of broken columns, it appeared as a glory to the old gods rather than an indication of the wealth of the tallest tower owners.

Over supper I asked Guido again about the One and the Many and while he meandered down labyrinthine Neoplatonic paths I took my own route into my heart and saw there the true nature of his discourse. What were all my lovers if not many manifestations of the One? Did not they all reflect my idea of what my imagination wanted, were they not all emanations from me?

My distraction was obvious.

"My dear Julia, I am boring you, Isabella would have shut me up a long time ago."

"No, not boring me, I was just thinking whether it was ironic or apt that as a painter of women's bodies you see the concept in metaphysical terms. I believe we realise it in the flesh, in sex."

Guido's face grew cloudy, "I do not understand."

I was bold with wine and the arrogance of youth; momentarily forgetting that I was merely voicing the philosophies of Mr C and that they were no more than words. But I fear I was seduced by the sound of my own voice.

"I believe it is like desire. You know, the blind wanting thing. Passion, lust, whatever you call it, we all feel it at some point in our lives."(And mine so long!). "It is a sign of our humanity as much as imagination or the thumb opposed to finger, something that sets us apart from every other creature moving on this earth. We think it is only elicited by people we love, but that isn't true. It is elicited by those who in some way conform to our ideal, in the Many we seek the One, the One we may never find."

Guido smiled, a touch patronisingly I thought.

"You are so young Julia, you have not yet met the One. He exists for you as surely as she existed for me."

"But I wonder if it matters, if the most important thing is the wanting. Perhaps the point of an ideal is that we never achieve it, not in this life. Surely that's what you mean by the Fire; we can only look at the shadows the flames cast on the wall, never at the source. Perhaps there is no ultimate ideal; perhaps it is only an idea each one of us has. It may be different for everyone, in the way that beauty is in the eye of the beholder, but we all have a dream, a fantasy to pursue."

I saw in my mind's eye Simonetta's lovely face and those of Mrs C and Luigi and Luigi's lips, the breadth of his shoulders and the globes of *David*'s arse – universal truths, if beauty is truth.

Guido was looking into the glass of Vernaccia before him, Michelangelo's favourite wine, and I heard his soft voice, "I found my One, I lived with my dream. It is possible."

He raised his head and smiled, "Do I look wistful now?"

I nodded and he leant back in his chair. He affected his quizzical air and looked at me down his long Roman nose, "If you don't believe there is a perfect partner for you why do you keep looking? I assume you are looking."

And how. It was my turn to smile, "I am an eternal optimist Guido."

We downed our espresso and drove back in the dark.

I stayed two more days in Florence, shopping and sightseeing, then headed for Milan with Guido's painting on the narrow back ledge of the Fiat and a vague yearning for something carnal. My intellect was sated, my head crammed full of images and words from Mr C's library and I still felt Guido's eyes on my skin. I drove to the mountains in pursuit of nature, my own.

Al Fresco

Mrs C had insisted I return via a different route, assuming my confidence – if not my driving skills – would be sufficiently improved to venture off the *autostrada*, not so far as to get myself lost but far enough to enjoy *la campagna*. My rustic experience included an overnight stay in a favourite haunt of hers, a *pensione* in a typically Tuscan hilltop village. I arrived at the *pensione* in the late afternoon, and a wonderfully gnarled old man, the patron, came to the front and beckoned me inside, saying his grandson would bring my luggage. He asked me where I had driven from and when I told him he shook his head in wonder. In truth I was dizzy with exertion and my limbs were shaking with exhaustion. The road had been in parts narrow and steep, rendering the drive and view a truly sublime event. I resolved to find a more suitable vehicle, like a tank, for my next venture into the thin air.

The old man continued, "*Lei e Milanese, signorina?*"

I was flattered to realise I had acquired a regional accent; to these speakers of the Lingua Franca I must have sounded like a cockney. I explained that I was English but lived in Milan as a teacher. I was here to enjoy the scenery.

The patron obviously approved. He was proud to have been born in this village and would die here, but the life was hard and the young people were moving away; the only income was from tourism. He was grateful to the many mad city dwellers who risked their lives on the roads to risk their necks on the pistes every Winter. Mrs C came annually for a couple of weekends when the snow fell, probably more for the *après-ski* than the exercise, but he had never seen the Fiat before. I was not surprised. There was scant room for a body; skis would have been a problem.

He chattered endlessly, and often incomprehensibly as he slipped into dialect, on the way to my room, the one Mrs C always used. It was large and bright and from the window you could see down the valley dotted with the red roofs of lower villages, above them the crest of the mountain Panna, so called because its naked rock face was the colour of cream.

The patron invited me to supper and said he would ask his grandson to join us. When I descended a few hours later on surer limbs I gave silent thanks to my friend – it seemed as if she had foreseen my every need. Lorenzo was handsome, perhaps younger than me, and just what I wanted.

He was awkward at first, rather shy but soon animated by what I was delighted to perceive as our mutual attraction. We spoke long into the evening, long after the patron had bidden us goodnight and long after it was proper that we should be alone. But I was a city girl, they would forgive me and frankly I did not care. We parted on the promise to meet the following afternoon when Lorenzo would take me to a magical place, his favourite space, somewhere I would never find on my own.

I stood in the doorway of my room. Someone had been to switch on the bedside light and turn down the covers. I breathed deeply, inhaling the cool green mountain air. I closed the door behind me and threw myself on the bed and pushed my face into the pillow to smell only the freshness of clean linen, not a note of Mrs C's scent. There was nothing in the room to suggest her presence, apart from me.

Had she brought Lorenzo here? Fucked him on this bed? Lorenzo had asked after Mrs C and I gathered that she usually came on her own, meeting up with friends who stayed in the next village. He gave no hint of anything other than a well-earned respect for my lover, who had helped him get the place in a Luccese college which he would take up in the Autumn.

He was, it transpired, two years younger than me, but I did not think age would be a deterrent to Mrs C's wishes, whatever they were or had ever been. She had wanted me, that much I knew, but whether I was one in a long line of lovers she took irrespective of age or gender, I never ascertained, not that I tried very hard. Mrs C was always quizzing me on my past and present sex life but never offered a history of her own beyond saying that she had been very young when she met Mr C, very young when she married him.

I kicked off my shoes, pulled my dress over my head and slipped under the covers into a long dreamless sleep.

The next day I was so excited at the prospective outing that the chosen means of transport caused me only momentary dismay. Lorenzo's shabby truck seemed even more unsuitable for the terrain than the Fiat, but I tucked myself in and gave my chauffeur a beatific smile.

We headed up to where the marble had been sliced from the mountains' flanks with thick wires, the blocks ranged along the route like massive white sentinels and I saw what Michelangelo must have seen when he journeyed into this wild place, the forms within the marble struggling to break free of its edges, breaking through into life. The scenery was stunning and so was the road.

Lorenzo wheedled his way round potholes and boulders, over humps and hillocks and I was shaken like a cocktail until I was as good as drunk. When we eventually pulled up at the mouth of the forest I could hardly stand. The clouds spun away above me and the earth quaked under my feet. I held on to the side of the truck while Lorenzo hurried round to take my hand and help me down on to the grass. I sat with my head between my knees while he unloaded the basket from the back seat and found some water which he must have poured onto a napkin and then laid on the exposed nape of my neck. He held it in place with one hand and gave me the bottle with the other, "*Allora, bevi Giulia, ti sentirai meglio.*"

The coolness on my neck and coursing down my throat did indeed stem the flow of nausea and when I looked into Lorenzo's handsome concerned face I knew I would soon be fine.

"Let's walk a little way into the forest," he said, "away from the road and then we can rest for a while, that is if you don't mind." He lifted the blanket, the basket and me, and kept hold of my hot hand as we walked between the trees. The air was fragrant with pine and the breeze high above in the tree tops filled it with sighs; singing wind cooled my skin and cleared my city-sullied senses. The terrain of the marble mountains was so austere and so savage that the pale colours of the forest, the slim, straight lines of the trees and the softness of the light falling through the lattice of branches seemed wonderfully calm and ordered.

We came to a small clearing and Lorenzo spread the blanket over the pale dry pine needles. He drew two chunky glasses from the basket and uncorked a bottle of ruby red wine from the family vineyards. We broke the coarse bread and cut the hard white cheese made from the sour milk of sheep. We tore the fat grapes from their frail stalks and spat the pips into the distance, laughing at our vulgarity. We differed on the technique for figs; Lorenzo simply pushed his thumbs against the flesh to split it, then turned the fruit inside out and tore the filaments from the pith with his bright teeth. I peeled off the thin layer of green and reached the pungent red fruit through the cream covering. We both drenched our hands and mouths in sticky juice and Lorenzo suggested we wash in the nearby stream.

I followed him faithfully deeper into the forest and soon became aware of a rushing sound, like the soughing of the leaves above us but higher and clearer and nearer. The stream was surprisingly wide and fast, swishing over the stones and through the exposed roots of the overhanging trees. I removed my shoes and manoeuvred my way down the bank to the water.

"*Stai attenta*, you will make wet your dress."

So I took the hem in my sticky hands and tucked it up around my knickers. Lorenzo had rolled his loose trousers up over his knees and laughing we lent down to rinse our hands and watch the pine needles shooting past our calves.

"If we walk a little further the stream opens up into a pool. Take my hand and take care to not slip on the stones."

He reached back to me and I took his now cool hand in mine, walking just a little way behind him, watching the stones under my tender feet, glancing up to see Lorenzo's dark hair curling over his collar, the wideness of his shoulders and his tight firm buttocks. I wanted him. I followed in a dream and was roused only on our arrival.

The bank suddenly became much steeper and we had to walk through a gully to get to the pool which appeared before us as a circle of light. The trees rose up around it but the branches did not overlap and I saw for the first time since we had entered the forest the brilliant cerulean of the sky. It was suddenly hotter, and when Lorenzo turned to smile at me I saw the beads of sweat forming on his upper lip.

"It is beautiful, no? Do you mind if I swim?"

I shook my head and he pulled off his shirt and flung it up the bank. I simply stared wholly unabashed at his magnificent torso, the skin so tanned by the sun and so firm with vigour I could barely restrain myself from reaching out to touch him. He felt my eyes upon him and smiled shyly, "I do not want to get my trousers wet, may I remove them?"

My throat too dry for words, I shrugged my shoulders and gave what I hoped was an indulgent smile. Heaven forbid that modesty should prevail! He turned his back to me and undid the buttons then lowered them over his beautiful buttocks. He wore nothing underneath, and as he bent down to pull them over his wet feet I glimpsed his prick hanging down in the triangle of his parted legs. He turned to walk backwards into the pool, beckoning to me, and like a beguiled damsel I waded in.

I felt the cold on my thighs and my dress grow heavy with water, then the cold in my cunt then around my waist and when the water reached my nipples he pulled me to him. The water between us took an age to part, a solid thing my breasts and jutting nipples cut through to reach the object of my desire. I wanted nothing between us so I heaved the sodden dress over my head, drenching my hair and my face, and flung it as far as I could up the bank. Then I reached down and dragged the wet band of my knickers to my ankles and flung them after my dress.

It was then I brought my body against his and felt the hardness of his prick against my belly, the cold smoothness of his skin on mine and his tongue in my mouth, our hands cutting through the silky water. And when we found the deepest part of the pool which covered me up to my chin and Lorenzo to his shoulders, he lifted my weightless body onto his prick and I floated upon him, my tongue deep in his mouth, my nipples against his chest, my arms around his neck. I had never felt so light, as if my body did not have any substance, as if I too were of water and although I could feel Lorenzo's prick inside me it was not the hot solid column I knew. I was full of the water, full of the sunlight pouring down on me. I pushed away from Lorenzo, who left me to float while holding on to my toes with their painted red petals of toenails. My breasts broke through the water and the sunlight kissed them, kissed my face and my belly just below the surface, then I felt a rush between my thighs as Lorenzo pulled me towards him. He walked between my legs and rested my thighs on his shoulders, sliding his hands along my back until I lay upon the water and his arms.

At first I could not tell the water from his tongue but then I knew its firmness and its sureness as he licked my sunning clitoris and delved underneath into the wet folds of my labia. I gave myself over wholly to the light and the sounds and the sense of the water and his tongue inside me. I came softly, like a ripple, but Lorenzo knew and lifted me out of the water and into his arms and up onto the bank. He lay me down on the soft needles and entered me so suddenly I thought it would all be over before I was dry. But no, he thrust into me gently and with tenderness, stopping to wipe the wet hair from my face, bending to lick the raised nipples that pushed into his chest, running his hands down my wet thighs. I could feel him this time, the fullness of his swollen prick, the warmth of his flesh in mine, the weight of his magnificent body on mine and I urged him to come in me, come hard in me.

He had been holding on only for my pleasure and he came at my bidding; I felt him spurting inside me, pouring into me like the stream. And as he lay upon my shoulder, catching his breath, I ran my hands down his wide back still glistening with the water and dappled with the light filtering down through the branches, and I wondered if anyone passed by whether they'd be able to make us out from the earth on which we lay. When Lorenzo pulled out of me I felt the semen seep out after him, onto the crushed needles beneath us.

"We must get back and dry off."

When we stood Lorenzo was at first amused and then alarmed at the crisscross of needles imprinted on my back and buttocks. I assured him they did not hurt but I slid into the water once more to wash them from my body while Lorenzo gathered up our clothes. He could not find my knickers. We slipped and laughed up the stream, holding on to our wet bundles and shoes and each other, naked but for the gold chain around my neck and the St Christopher hanging by a silver thread from Lorenzo's.

We found our way back to the blanket and the basket, and while our clothes lay drying on stones in a small patch of sunlight falling between the branches we lay down. Lorenzo slept while I listened to the sounds of the forest and felt the arms of this man around me and smelt the warm skin of his chest under my cheek.

I must have grown lonely and wanted to wake him so I gently unlaced myself from his arms and slid down his belly to his groin, where his penis was small and soft on the cushion of his balls. I lifted it in my hand and lowered my lips to kiss its red head. Lorenzo sighed above me, deep in sleep, and I took his penis in my mouth, gently sucking on it like a thumb, curling my tongue around it and over it until I felt it growing like magic; it filled my mouth and I had to draw back my head or I would have choked on its length. I felt Lorenzo's hands in my hair, I heard his breath deep and slow and I sensed the veins rising on the side of his penis, the blood rushing to its tip, swelling it. I tasted the familiar saltiness and drew back before he came.

I rose up and spread my thighs over him, my cunt wet as water, and he slipped inside me with ease and clasped my waist. I closed my eyes and threw back my head to feel the light through the branches flickering on my face. I raised my arms and lifted the still damp hair from my neck and knew my breasts looked magnificent to Lorenzo beneath me. But I was only aware of my body and my pleasure, even his prick inside me was my prick, the hands upon my body were part of me, the light on my skin, the scents in the air, the sounds all around and the very breeze that brought them to me were me and existed only for me and because of me to make love to me.

As I felt the upward rush against my cervix I felt as if I had fucked the earth and this body beneath me was only a part of that earth. I wanted to keep on coming, clutching at the column of our flesh. Lorenzo called my name and I opened my eyes, dazzled with the sense of my own grandeur and dizzy with sensation. He was smiling, mystified but content and I rose off him and stood over him, my cunt a blowsy rose, the semen slipping down my leg.

"Such a beautiful thing," he murmured as he pulled himself up to kiss the still visibly rampant bud of my clitoris, grasping my thighs and adding his fingerprints to the marks of pine needles and grass on my soft flesh. His tongue was quick and sweet and I came again, but it was a shallow experience in comparison.

I walked over to the stone and donned my damp dress; I flung Lorenzo's clothes to him and packed up the basket, swigging the last of the warm wine from the bottle. We drove back to the village in silence, the windows down and the wind rushing in. As my dress dried upon my hot body I felt the cold of the evening creeping in and watched the horizon grow rosy along the ridge of mountains on either side of the valley. I sensed Lorenzo's bewilderment but could do no more than place my hand on his thigh, leaving it there for the entire journey. When he stopped outside the *pensione* he turned to me as if to speak but I laid my finger across his lips.

I closed the truck door and walked round to his side and through the open window I kissed his cheek, "*Ciao, Lorenzo, e grazie.*"

He said nothing but looked straight ahead and drove off. I did not hear him return that night. I left very early the next morning.

I tore down the *autostrada* as if a long lost love had been found and was waiting for me at the other end. Oblivious to the beauty that had accosted my senses for more than a week and looking neither left nor right, I stopped only for the toll gates and to refuel the car and myself in a cool *Pavesi* from where I called Mrs C; I knew she would not stay long in the South. I sang along to the now familiar songs in the tape deck as the car chewed up the miles between the mountains and the plain, occasionally glancing at myself in the rear view mirror to catch my altered state. I felt the sun under my skin, the cold streams rushing through my veins and the sweet fresh air of mountains in my lungs but I was anxious already to be back. As the afternoon sun hit the mid-point of my vision I saw the concrete towers that formed the outskirts of Milan.

I parked the magical machine and took the lift to the penthouse where Mrs C was waiting for me with wine and food. I ate in excited mouthfuls as I recounted the sights of my trip and the details of my purchases. She was happy with her present and much amused at my day as an artist's model, but when I showed her the painting she grew quiet.

"Isn't it wonderful? Does it look like me? Am I so very beautiful?"

She nodded without taking her eyes from the paper.

"Well, it is you who made me beautiful; I never felt it before that day, that day when you said I was your Venus."

She raised her lovely head and turned her dark eyes on me and I knew her affection was deep – this woman loved me, loved me more than I could ever love her. She loved me as a part of herself, as a daughter of her desire, a child of her imagination.

"No *cara*, you were always beautiful, and you will become more so."

She made to give me back the painting but I told her to keep it and remember me as I would always like to be remembered. She smiled indulgently, "You sound like an old woman, but really it is only the very young who can speak like that. At sixteen I thought myself so wise, so weary, as if the world had nothing new to show me. But then I met Claudio."

Mr C was rarely mentioned by name.

"Lorenzo sends his regards."

Mrs C lowered her eyes and nodded, then ran her fingers over the pale washes of the watercolour, "Thank you for this, I will – how do you say? Treasure it."

There was sadness in her voice and I wonder now if I had been her magic glass, as in a fairy tale. If when she looked in the mirror she saw not her reflection but a younger, fresher, fairer image, one that she had created. Unable to reinvent herself she had invented me. In me she gave herself, to Lorenzo, to her husband. And her husband? What had he given his wife?

I kissed her cheek and wished her goodnight. My bags were heavy so I took a taxi to my apartment where I flung myself on the bed and felt the wheels of the car spinning beneath me as I rushed into dreams.

Americano

The weeks that followed my return to the city were the same shape as before but the texture was different. The light was still strong but the sun seemed lower. In the evenings I took to wearing a jacket. I even disentangled my suspender belts and stockings to cover my smooth brown legs and slipped back into the shoes I had abandoned for the strappy sandals of Summer. The days were warm and the tourists wandered around in their halter necks and shorts but the *conoscenti* understood. I was however, dismayed to see that the new colours were olive and mustard and determined to stay in the pastels of the hot months as long as possible.

I felt a nostalgia for the Summer. It was as if I were gone already, as if I had already said goodbye. And then I met the American.

I had stopped outside Valentino's to admire the fabulous dress in the window. It was an evening gown of purple velvet. The strapless bodice was embroidered with fine gold thread and a dark red jewel glowed in the dip of the neckline between the mannequin's perfectly spherical breasts.

A man stopped beside me and I was surprised to hear the accent in "*Lei sarebbe bellisima in un vestito così.*"

I responded in the Queen's English, "Any woman would look beautiful in such a dress" and turned towards the Mid-West sound. I was pleasantly surprised by a fair-haired man with light blue eyes and an easy smile, well-dressed in a loose, almost careless way, his obviously Armani jacket falling from insouciant but broad shoulders.

"I should have known, you don't quite look Italian."

"And you certainly don't sound Italian."

"Well, I'm only a visitor, here for the shows."

Twice a year the streets of Milan ran like rivers swollen by the flood of journalists and buyers from the rest of the hopeful sartorial world. You could tell them apart from the usual shoppers by the garlands of cameras they raised to every window – the Japanese were the most trigger-happy, shooting not only the clothes but the shoes and accessories, even the household goods.

"This is going to sound rather forward but I'm here on my own. If you can spare the time could we have a drink some place? I'd sure appreciate the company."

I was on my way to an empty room so I agreed and he led me to a tiny bar down a side street I had never noticed before. I gathered he knew Milan well. In fact he was almost as in love with the place as I. He worked for an American fashion magazine and attended the shows not so much for the clothes as for the opportunity to visit Italy and presumably to importune young girls, not that he was very much older than me. His directness was startling and then rather refreshing. He asked me so many questions about myself I lost all sense of propriety and simply told him the truth, not that in retrospect I would have lied but perhaps I should have been a little less forthcoming.

I spent so much time with Italians and spoke so simple an English with my students that I was glad to use my mothertongue for talk of the things I loved. I spoke of huge ideas in the way only the young can speak of them, with an optimism and arrogance that such things could be achieved, that I would indeed achieve them. He rolled a cigarette in black liquorice paper and smiled. We spoke of England and America and again of me. His attention was charming and complete – several *aperitivi* were downed and two hours passed before the darkness outside dimmed in any way the brightness of my chatter and the warmth of his smile. He asked me to join him for supper but I declined, it was almost too much too soon. Twenty-four hours seemed a decent but not punishing interval and I agreed to meet him the following evening.

The thought of the American floated in and out of my consciousness all morning and when I met Megan for lunch in the Galleria she noted my high colour and my distraction. I told her about my new friend, what little there was to tell.

"Good lord Jools, you'll be picking them up on street corners next."

"He's interesting."

"Interesting?" Megan could make any reasonable explanation seem the most improbable thing this side of sanity.

"Well," she sighed, "You need something to take your mind off that Luigi, but I do hope you're not intending to fall in love with someone who's likely to abscond to another continent tomorrow."

"I'm meeting him tonight."

"Like I said, tomorrow. Mind you, the quick exit is no bad thing. I often wonder if the only way to stay in love is to end it, you know, avoid the disappointment, the habit."

"Megan, how did you get to be so old?"

"Old? No, cynical perhaps, although maybe you have to be old to be cynical. I just don't believe in falling in love, do you?" She turned her sharp grey eyes on me.

"I don't know, I could be tempted."

Megan raised her ruby red aperitif. "Here's to love, and temptation." She mentioned the American no more, neither did I.

But the American stayed with me for the rest of the day. I saw his smile before me, heard his soft slow vowels, I even fancied that I could taste the memory of his liquorice cigarette, smelt it in my hair. My students found me distant and undemanding. Seven o'clock found me in the empty bar.

I was pretending to read a book when I felt his hand on my shoulder, felt its warmth. He sat down opposite and ordered an *aperitivo*, then a focaccia brimful of mozzarella and avocado and tomato and fragrant with herbs. I nibbled on a brioche, strangely and immediately depressed by the advent of food that suggested the offer of supper would not be repeated. The American explained that he had not had time to eat all day nor would he later. "I'll make it up to you," he said.

Embarrassed that my feelings were so very obvious and having given so much of myself away the evening before I determined to take something from this time and this man and began to question him as intensely as he had me, but it seemed I had had all I was going to get of his life, past and present.

"You're not a drug dealer are you?" I was only half joking.

"Heavens no, why should you think that?" He laughed.

"You seem to have something to hide." I may have coloured at my impertinence.

"No, I have something to discover, I have you. I know all about me, I don't know you and I want to. Yet I wonder how much of you is possible to know."

"You have only to ask."

"That's not what I mean." He looked down at his watch and grimaced. He had to go. A hot disappointment shot through me and quivered behind my eyes which were suddenly brimming with tears.

"This is beginning to sound like a movie, but can we meet tomorrow? Same place same time?"

I kept my head lowered and said, "If it's the movie I know, it has an unhappy ending."

"But romantic."

It could have been a question, but what of romance, what did I know of romance? I knew it was always appended to love, romantic love, and what did I know of that? To be 'in love' – a *banal grandeur* or a grand banality? From the outside it seemed like an excuse for bad behaviour, for fine minds distracted from a higher purpose, or perhaps it was the higher purpose: it had led Dante to Paradise. And from the inside?

Of course I agreed to meet the American again and he took my hand and touched my fingertips to his lips, and the dam of my disappointment burst and the blood flooded to those tips and tingled and burned under the skin.

"*A domani,*" he said and departed in an almost indecent haste, thrusting several notes into the patron's hand on his way out.

I found it hard to sleep that night, going over the American's words and deeds, my responses to them, knowing that somehow we had crossed a border, but to what country of the body and mind exactly I did not know. Frantic with tiredness, anxiety and excitement I hurried through the next day, aware that I was definitely too eager for the night and to find myself again in the nameless bar down the quiet side street.

He was waiting and rose to greet me, not with the customary peck on both cheeks but with a soft kiss on my breathless mouth. Any doubt as to our destination dissolved on his lips – now I understood. There would be no more niceties, no more talk of grand designs. I was the grand design.

He helped me out of my jacket and led me to the table where the Prosecco was misting the two unusually fine glasses. He sat down opposite and, handing me a glass, said, "You have beautiful breasts, I can see your nipples through the silk of your blouse."

I can't recall if I blushed but as I raised the slippery vessel to my lips I could not prevent my hand from shaking. The wine fizzed over my fingers, the table and my blouse. The patron brought a cloth for the table and a napkin for me, and as I wiped it over the dampness my American friend told me again I had beautiful breasts. Mr Parola was not the only one of my students to have whispered such extravagant compliments and I had feigned ignorance of their Italian but this was my language, I understood and acknowledged every word. I wanted this man as much as he wanted me.

He took the napkin from my still trembling hands and began to draw it slowly over my breasts, it seemed a long time but it was probably only a moment before he let the napkin drop into my lap. I kept my head lowered and watched as his hands continued to move. Perhaps I felt that if I didn't see anyone else, no one would see me – perhaps there was no one else in the bar, perhaps it didn't really exist outside of our meetings. I felt the warmth of his hands and the hardness of his palms against my nipples and I resented the remaining layers between his skin and mine. He kneaded my breasts through the silk and I think I heard his voice reiterating his observation – yes, indeed I had beautiful breasts – over and over, until his words made me wet and my breathing grew shallow and hard.

Suddenly he stopped and I watched through lowered eyes as he retrieved the napkin from my lap, folded it and placed it on the table, next to the necessary lire which he drew from his pocket.

"Here, give me your hands."

He helped me stand and into my jacket and with his arm around my shoulders led me into the street, now dark with the evening and a solitary streetlamp. Only shadows fell through the windows of the bar which did in fact seem empty, even of the patron.

I was not surprised when he pushed me against the wall, not hard but with enough force to feel the brick through my clothing. His mouth pushed against mine as I felt his prick hard against my belly. Between our lips he murmured, "I want to see your breasts, I want to see how beautiful they are." His hands moved to my damp blouse, undid the buttons from my neck to my waist then slipped inside, all the while I was pinioned against the wall by his prick pushing through the fabric of his trousers to hold my body fast.

He slid his hands around to my back and unfastened my bra, the cups of which he pushed up over my so fulsome breasts. Only then did he stop kissing me and stood back a little – he was looking at my breasts, shining in the light of the only streetlamp and of his admiration. He took each nipple between his thumb and forefinger and pulled them gently until they had grown almost impossibly long, then he bent his head to suck them, and I closed my eyes, shutting out the possibility that we might be seen, that someone would pass by – I gave myself over to the heat of this man's mouth and found myself rushing down the sensational paths that led from my breasts to my cunt. Like some electrical circuit that connected my nipples to my clitoris I was so switched on I felt as if the whole of Milan could have been plunged into darkness and my body would shine and its light would fall on the burnished head at my breasts, but for now the dark sufficed to hide us both.

Had he continued for much longer I would have come but he withdrew his mouth and said, "I want to taste you, I want to know how you taste," and knelt down before me. I opened my eyes to see my American in his immaculately suited knees before me on the cobblestones, like some penitent before his saviour, but I was no saint and he was no martyr, he was my devotee.

He slipped his hands up my stockinged legs, up to the naked skin of my thighs and drew down the now drenched knickers to my heels. I lifted first one Ferragamo-shod foot then the other to facilitate their removal and smiled when I saw him put them in his jacket pocket. He pushed up my skirt and I looked down to see his head drawing to my cunt.

How many mouths, how many tongues have conversed with me this way? But this man was not merely a good after-dinner-speaker, he was a gourmet and my cunt was his *antipasto*, *primo piatto*, *secondo* and *dolce*. He made a feast of me on the trestle table of the alley. He licked me and sucked me until in the dull air I heard the sound of his tongue in my wetness like a cat lapping cream.

He did not penetrate me but caressed my clitoris so constantly I felt that part of me would penetrate him, fill his mouth like some magical prick, burst into him in a shower of myself. I put my hands upon his head in benediction and I came like a god. All the breath, the air, the light went out of me and I opened my eyes not into the temple of my senses but the dark alley. The cold touched my naked skin and I was aware once more of the brick wall at my back and in understanding my own discomfort grew alarmed for my lover, for the stones under his knees.

"You must stand, the ground is so hard."

He rose before me and drew his body to mine. His lips were shiny in the streetlight and when he kissed me I tasted myself in his mouth. It was different to the taste of me on Mrs C, perhaps the sharpness of his aftershave and slight sweet liquorice confused the femaleness but I kissed him back and pushed my tongue between his teeth as surely as he had his into my cunt.

I felt him still hard against me and waited for the undoing of his trousers, for him to fuck me up against the wall like a whore, like the young ones with nowhere to go and the need in them strong. But he simply kissed me and held me and made no move to free his prick and in truth I was glad. It was over for me. He would wait and I would have to wait to feel him inside me, to know me.

"We must go now. I have to get back to the hotel."

He smoothed down my skirt and smoothed back the stray hair from my face. He rubbed his thumb gently around my mouth to remove the red that had smeared over the distinct line of my lips which he softly kissed one last time. I smelt myself on him and licked my juice from his face and combed my fingers through his pale hair. He brushed the damp dirt off his knees then put his arm around my shoulder. He slipped his free hand into his pocket but did not give me back my knickers and I did not ask.

We surfaced into the night street and walked a way along it until we found a taxi. On the way to my apartment he asked if I would spend the following evening with him. Again I agreed but not to the bar, there was no going back. He took my telephone number. He said he would call at six and to be waiting. I was.

At 6 'o clock precisely his slinky transatlantic drawl slid down the phone like an offer I could not refuse, "Just dress casual, something simple, but no underwear. A taxi will collect you in 15 minutes."

I laughed as if his request were rather silly but in truth I was as wet as the ocean that divided his kind from mine and as I lowered the phone I pulled down my black knickers and unhooked the black satin bra I was wearing. The fine lace top stockings I left gently grooved into the soft flesh of my thighs. The American had interrupted my toilette but I continued painting my lips, brushing my hair into a pleat and misting my entire body with cologne from the crystal flacon Mrs C had given me. I donned a plain black dress, pulled on my uncasually high black shoes, threw a shawl around my shoulders and entered the lift which shuddered down to the ground floor where the taxi was waiting.

I felt the cold leather under my thighs, and had I been in the dark of a black London cab I think I would have raised my skirt so there would be nothing between me and the seat, in homage to O, naked already, but I folded my hands in my lap and contented myself with memories of American kisses, memories that in effect blinded me to the journey. I was not even aware the car had stopped until the door was opened and I found myself outside an ornate doorway.

The porter ushered me through the luscious vestibule and into the waiting lift. He reached in to press the floor button and placed a gold room key in my hand. As he stood back with a smile the doors closed – too late I noticed how beautiful he was. I felt the rush of the ascent as a rush of excitement in my veins and when the lift opened into a wide corridor lined with huge blue ceramic vases full of exotic flowers I wondered if at the door to room 26 I might be greeted by Concetta. I did know that whoever opened the door, he or she would see an assured young woman, brimful of elan and not the shy girl who had contemplated flight outside her student's penthouse.

But no one answered to my knocking, and I had to admit myself with the key. The room more than fulfilled my expectations. While the rest of Milan was paring down to minimalist proportions of black and white and concealed lighting this hotel was reinventing Rococo. The light of the chandelier was fascinated in the myriad crystal drops and reflected in the gilt-edged mirror running the length of one wall above a lacquered wood sideboard. On this was circled a fabulous gold necklace with gems the colour of claret and in its centre a pair of earrings in the form of inverted gold fleurs de lys with the same red gems like petrified wine dripping from each point.

On the huge bed lay the gown from Valentino. I shrugged my black silk slip to the floor and stepped into purple folds of velvet and gold. I pulled it up over my hips from which the skirt fell like a hot night, drew the boned bodice up over my breasts and reached round to slide the tiny black hooks into the tiny black eyes that ran down my spine from under my shoulder blades to my waist. I was supple and dextrous and soon cinctured as firmly and tenderly as in a lover's arms. I had no need of a bra; the bodice grasped my breasts and pushed them upward in an astonishing display of grandeur.

I walked to the mirror to admire the effect and to don the jewels. Such a pretty woman, where was my charming man? While I was clasping the necklace the American entered with armsful of black velvet which he flung upon the bed. As it billowed across the counterpane I recognised the cape that had been spread in a circle at the foot of the mannequin. He walked up behind me and in the reflection before me I saw the embodiment of my desire – this tall, fair man in his evening suit, his soft hair falling on the wing-collar of his white shirt, the dark green papillon tied under his sharp chin like an invitation to my undoing.

I did not turn as he came up close and placed his cool hands on my neck and slid them down my arms – I stared before me into the mirror and watched the reflection of my own seduction. He brought his head down onto the white arch of my shoulder and took the soft skin in his mouth and licked it and sucked it till I feared he would mark me, but the sensation was so sweet I let him continue his way up my neck and across my back to the other side. As he kissed my skin, so thin I could see the blue veins pulsing across the pale expanse, he drew his hands back up my arms and over my breasts, as ripe as grapes in the purple velvet of the bodice. He ran his fingers over my nipples, standing proud through the fabric and slipped them along the edges where the bones of the underlying corset pressed into the softness.

All the while I had reached behind me to find his zip which I lowered, and released the long, hard prick. He moved his hands down and raised the heavy folds of my skirt – I saw him smile when he encountered my naked behind. I felt his prick searching out my cunt, now as slippery as the lilac satin lining that cascaded over my hips. I had to raise myself slightly, even on my towering heels, but I felt him plunge into me with the sureness of lust and pushed against him, my arms outstretched on the sideboard. He circled my waist with one arm, so tightly I could hardly breathe, the other he pushed under the folds of the gown and his fingers delved in the velvet to find my clitoris.

I watched us in the mirror – bent at the waist and my head raised, I saw the darkness around my aureoles as my nipples threatened to break free of the restraining bodice with every thrust and I saw my lover behind me, such sternness upon his face, as hard as the prick he was thrusting into me between the soft globes of my arse.

I stared at him, dared him to look at me and when his eyes met mine in the glass we knew together the voluptuous pleasure of our mutual seduction, the high drama of the act both performed and witnessed by ourselves. The duplicity was astounding and so European. I knew nothing of the Americas or their inhabitants but I knew this man to be as sophisticated and decadent as the Corallos; his fair open air was American, his luxurious sexuality was of this land. He and I were foreigners but we had embraced Italy so tightly we had somehow slipped under its skin. In the mirror I saw a Medici princess, at my back the Machiavellian prince who would fuck me forever.

His fingers quickened over my clitoris as he hurried his push into my cunt. I watched our faces change with the onset of our orgasm, watched the pink rise over my breasts and the sweat break through between them and over my upper lip. We came together and when the flood of semen broke through the dam of his softening prick I turned my face to his and kissed his mouth and the semen flowed down my thighs and over the tops of my stockings into the black mesh.

He broke for air first and told me we should go, we had tickets for the opera. But of course. I knew *Don Giovanni* was playing for the first time in seasons and that tickets had been sold out for months, but it seemed fitting on such a night that some sort of magic had been practised. As I reapplied my lipstick the fine high notes of Donna Elvira's exquisite lamentation on the ungrateful soul who betrays her rose in my memory until they slipped from my glossy mouth in a whisper.

The American had not heard me, he was opening the champagne which had been cooling in a silver ice-filled bowl on a low table in front of the window. He drew back the brocade drapes and I half-expected to see the lawns of the Boboli Gardens outside instead of the bright lights of a twentieth century city; to hear the clop of horses' hooves in the street below where the Ferraris roared and the Porsches purred. I was in another time, my lover was in another place.

"The view from the Metropole is stunning, great towers of light, buildings so high the tops really are in the clouds. You should come with me to America. Come live with me in America. You would love it – so different. Europe is dying, what you love about it is that it is dying, decadent – like a rose in full bloom its perfume is strong but it can only wither. In America everything is new, like hope, everything is possible. Yes, we are cunning, yes we are corrupt, but in the way of children, we're fooling no one, not even ourselves.

"This place is romantic, but New York is sexy. This country is full of *roues*, of Don Giovannis and Casanovas, well-versed in the art of love, but old. They have style but they lack energy. You have both, you are so young and so beautiful – I will lay my city at your feet like a velvet cloak. Come with me."

"I just might." I may even have meant it.

I downed the champagne with a rather theatrical flourish and the American swung the velvet cape around me. We descended to the street and into the waiting car and this time I felt the cool satin under my thighs as we sped towards La Scala, the music already beating in my veins.

The night seemed to dissolve, no sequence, only sensations. I heard voices, music, his voice. I felt his breath on my neck as he drew near to whisper obscenities in the *entr'acte*. I felt his fingers on my skin before they touched me, I was magnetised by his closeness and the distance of his body from mine. I could hardly breathe for the sounds in the air, so high I had to strain for their understanding. I could not think for the pull of my blood rushing towards his, not move for drowning in the rivers of Babylon coursing down my legs.

The champagne sparkled in my head, the mirrors in the restaurant dazzled with my reflection and his voice, always his voice and the hot words he poured over my skin. The kisses he placed on my wrist like cool perfume and on the softness of my arms curving to his across the white linen of the tablecloth. Then the sheets flung back and our bodies naked between them. His skin on mine a revelation, richer than velvet and smoother than satin. I wanted to be under him, inside him, behind his smile, on the other side of his kiss.

Our voices dry with talking and the champagne gone, he kissed me goodnight and fell to sleep, as must I have done as the pale thin light slipped between the dark velvet drapes. When I awoke he was not beside me. The bed was warm, his clothes were all around, but he was not there. I had been roused by a knocking at the door and at my sleepy bidding the beautiful young man from the lobby entered in an aroma of coffee and hot brioche.

I pulled the sheet up over my nakedness as he placed the tray next to me, next to the empty crystal glasses and the now dull red roses from a gypsy on the steps of the opera house. He bowed and departed and I rose into what suddenly registered as a work day.

Showered and coffeed I put on my discarded black dress and shoes and found my shawl in the twist of far flung covers. I wrote "Thank you" on a sheet of hotel paper and placed it on the sideboard under the necklace I had worn all night and whose shape was embossed on my neck for the rest of that long day.

I took my purse and a taxi to my room and as I was changing into more suitable teaching garb a driver arrived at my door with a huge black box, a golden V embossed on its lid. I opened it to find the dress and the jewellery but no note. I told the man, "This is not mine. Please take it back, the gentleman will understand."

Home Again

There was no time for reflection. I rushed into my day with an energy that surprised me because I could not possibly have had any left. Maybe habit intervened to carry me from Via Tortona to Piazza Bracca, from bored mistress to sanguine child, since I certainly was not there. Every thought in my head, every atom of my body was with the American.

My students seemed unusually proficient, or perhaps I was not so exacting, but the day was long and I was glad of its end. I had arranged to meet Megan for supper in a *Spaghetteria* that served five courses of pasta, one of them blue. It was over the third course, the *vongole*, that I gave in to her questions as to the reason for my rosy cheeks, dark-shadowed eyes and constant lapses of concentration. I told my curious friend of my lover, lately absconded to the other side of the Atlantic (what he had referred to as 'the culture gap') and waited for her response, wondering whether it would be patronising or censorious.

She simply said, "Do you think you'll see him again?"

"No."

"I'm so sorry Jools."

I was taken aback by the genuine concern in her voice. I knew she cared for me, but raised under the harshest of emotional regimes she considered it indulgent to cry over spilt semen.

She said nothing for a while and kept her eyes lowered as she reached across the table to take my hand, tapping idly beside my untouched plate. When she looked up she was smiling and called for the waiter, "Ancora piu di vino."

I waited until Megan was safely on the last tram home and wandered back to the square on a long, circuitous route as was my wont. I was walking slowly past the church, looking down at the cobblestones and kicking away the remembered folds of velvet that had swished around my sparkling feet the night before when a hand from the shadows wiped the smile from my enraptured face.

I think my heart stopped. In the silence of the missed beat I heard, "*Ciao bella*," and felt the hot whiskeyed breath against my ear.

"I've been waiting for you, waited here all night. What an alley cat you are, lucky I'm a tom."

"What do you want Jack?"

"Why, you of course."

I was relieved, for a moment. "Well you can't have me."

"That's what you think."

"That's what I know Jack. Please just go home and leave me alone."

"I can't do that Jools."

Quicker than a thought he had his hands around my neck and pulled me, almost lifted me, against him and crushed his lips against mine. He sought to push his tongue between them, grinding his teeth into the soft skin so hard I tasted blood in my mouth. I thought I would suffocate but had a more rational idea and raised my knee to his groin. He sensed its elevation and drew back immediately, keeping me literally at his long arm's length, his hands still at my throat. I seized his wrists and drew them down while he snorted in an unconvincing attempt at derision.

"Playing hard to get? Well, I'm game for anything."

"Jack you're mad, you're drunk. Please go home and we'll talk about this tomorrow."

He turned his head towards the gleaming clock face on the church tower and then back to me, "In a few minutes it will be tomorrow, but I don't want to talk to you, just fuck you."

"And I just want you to go."

"If that's what you really want."

"It is."

"Have it your way, for now."

He stood resolutely still but pulled a slim, no doubt real, gold lighter and case from his inside pocket and drew out a cigarette. The blue light of the flame played across his heavy features to intended sinister effect. He took a long, almost theatrical drag on the cigarette and clicked the case and the lighter shut. I was shaking inside and Jack knew. He raised his head and exhaled into the darkness above me.

"I have a message for you, from a – how should I say? – mutual friend."

He paused to give me sufficient time to realise we could indeed have a few.

"He's looking forward to seeing you at his club; in fact he was rather hoping I would bring you along some time."

He took one last drag and threw the cigarette onto the cobblestones where it continued to smoulder in the shadow of his departing form. Only when he was quite out of sight did I put my key in the lock. I was momentarily overwhelmed by the anxiety the encounter had induced in me, then angry at my foolishness for surely fear of Jack was laughable, but I could not sleep, not alone.

I do not know how I would have responded had her husband answered my call but Mrs C's voice, albeit brusque with concern, was welcome to my ears.

"Concetta is here but otherwise yes, I am alone."

She offered to send her driver – was she shameless or just too kind? But I insisted that I would find my own way.

I washed Jack's cologne from my face and hands and pulling a shawl around my shoulders I re-entered the night to make my way to Via Monte Napoleone. I kept my eyes on the cobblestones, my steps were sure and fast. I did not feel the rough wind that had risen and tugged at my hair, the emptiness of the streets was a vacancy in my consciousness – *sempre senza paura*, Mrs C had said, *è questo che amo di te*. Yet I was afraid, afraid of my ignorance, of my lover's duplicity, of my loss of any approximation to the understanding of things as they really were, or indeed if they were real. I feared what I was forcing, an inevitable confrontation, but was more afraid of being alone with the questions, knowing they would not still in my head until answered. I would never know for sure why the American had done as he did, but I would know how far Mrs C was implicated in her husband's entertainment business. Jack's meaning had been clear enough through the fug of his alcohol and dope. He could take me to a place that I had been close to accepting as a figment of an imagination, mine or Mr C's, unreal. But it was real, here and now in Milan; perhaps a baroque brothel, of which Mrs C's boudoir was no doubt a pale imitation. A hall of mirrors reflecting an endless debauchery fading into a *fin de siècle* satiety. And the procuress? The possibility of her complicity was more than I could bear and I strode towards her in bewildered fury.

I was dishevelled when I entered the bright lobby, my hair mussed by the wind, my face shiny and red, but the night porter merely tipped his cap to me and called the lift. Anger had impelled me to this point, only confusion stood between me and tears when I reached the top. Mrs C opened the golden door.

"*Giulia*! What is the matter my love?"

"Where is he, your husband?"

"What do you want with my husband *Giulia*?"

She seemed more fearful than suspicious. She lifted my chin on her fingertips, "Look at me *cara*, tell me what is wrong. I can help you, surely I can help you."

I looked into her eyes. They seemed as they had always seemed, dark and kind and concerned, no menace, no lies, just me.

"Yes, you can."

Mrs C opened her arms and took me in. She did not ask any more questions but led me to the bedroom and bade me undress and slip between the silky sheets, still warm from her recently risen body.

She left me only to return soon after with a pale golden liquid fizzing in a gold rimmed goblet which she raised to my lips – "to calm you," she said. It was sweet and cool and the bubbles lifted my spirits and lowered my pulse. I felt safe once again. She placed the empty goblet on the frilly bedside table and lay down beside me to draw me to her. She brought her lips to mine and kissed me so softly it was like whispering.

I opened her hastily donned gown and sensed her quiver under my cold fingertips. I moved them down and slipped them into her wet cunt. I wanted to put all of me in her, my whole body in that warm vermillion space but for now I pushed as much of me as she could take until she murmured against my lips "*Basta*," and I withdrew my slippery fingers and ran them up to her breasts and circled the nipples with her juice. I lowered my head and sucked first gently then hard until they were as tumescent as pricks.

"You will hurt me tonight," said my lover. "You want to hurt me."

She was smiling but perhaps she was right.

"You are too rough, I will be more gentle. Let me make love to you."

And she moved her lips down my body, licking me and kissing me and taking tiny pieces of my skin into her mouth to suck into rosy buds, marking my body with circles of pinkness for days afterwards. When she reached my cunt she paused and raised her eyes to mine. I looked down to see her face a shining moon in the dark sky of her hair which brushed against my belly like a million kisses.

She smiled again and said "How beautiful," and turned her head to kiss my cunt, to press her lips against those lips as if they were a mouth. I felt her tongue delving in between them, cool and firm and withdrawing to lick backwards and forwards. And then she was between my thighs, her head a dark mass on my groin and she raised her head again that I might see her, and I saw her black eyes and her mouth shiny in the soft lamplight and I saw her tongue like a wide red prick in my cunt.

I bade her lie beside me so that I might kiss her cunt while she kissed mine and we lay along each other, our lacquered fingernails curving crescent moons into the hemispheres of each other's arses and our tongues lapping in unison in the folds of our cunts. Her dark hair and my blonde tresses fell like night and day across our bodies, Sera and Alba, evening and dawn making love across the dreamscape of night.

I finally slept in Mrs C's arms, inhaling her scent and that of our sex. I slept until the morning when I was woken by my lover's kisses on the top of my bent head and the aroma of coffee wafting through the room.

"Concetta has brought us breakfast, come sit up and put on this gown."

I slipped my arms into a glorious robe of Chinese silk, and while the dragon chased its tail down my back we broke brioche into the sheets and laughed at each other's milky moustaches.

"I see you are feeling much better now, do you want to tell me what happened last night?"

My lightness burst in an instant, "I don't think I can, do you mind?"

"That is obviously irrelevant."

"I'm sorry."

She pouted and looked into the pale brown coffee, visible now she had spooned the froth into my mouth. She seemed hurt, and perhaps she had just cause.

But what could I do? I could not believe, did not want to believe, that this woman wanted to share me with the members of her husband's club, and yet it was she who had introduced me to her husband, handed me over. Had I disappointed her too? Failed her? If she did not know about the abortive visit and Jack's importuning I would not be the one to tell her, if she did it would mean that she was the one in control, the one pulling all the strings, from the edges of Jack's leer to the straps of the vertiginous shoes I had donned for the American.

Mrs C lifted her head and turned to me with her beatific smile, "No, there is no need to explain. I want only to help you if you are in need."

It was my turn to avert my eyes, "I want to go home." The words had left my mouth before I had time to realise they were suddenly true.

Mrs C was still for a while, then drew her knees up under her chin and tilted her head, her whole body a question that she was too discreet to ask. "Yes, perhaps you should go away, but only for a while, only until you feel better. Perhaps a few weeks at home will do you good. I know you are homesick."

Yes, I was homesick, I longed for the huge embrace of my family, for the Surrey flowerbeds, for the view from Waterloo Bridge, for strong tea made with water that left a brown film clinging to the side of the pot.

"Yes, you must go home, that is where you belong for the present. You will be home tomorrow."

"And all I have to do is click my red heels?"

The allusion was lost on my lovely purveyor of shoes, none so vulgar as Dorothy's.

"If you want to go, you can go now."

I was suddenly piqued at the lack of argument, of any attempt to persuade me to stay. "And Susan? My students?"

"*Ci penso io*" – leave it to me.

"But I don't want to leave you," I realised that I meant it and the pain of our threatened separation was already rising in my chest.

She brushed my fringe to one side and kissed my forehead and I felt her lips moving against my skin, "You will never do that."

But she had known, as surely as Luigi, that I would have to go some day, so why not now? It was almost as if she had been waiting for me to raise the subject. She wrapped her arms around me and the sadness fell between us like a wall.

I had promised Megan only recently that I would not leave without telling her. When I returned to Santo Spirito after my morning lessons I called her and we arranged to meet in the Galleria. She wasn't surprised at my news.

"I'll miss you but I understand Jools, really I do. And don't worry about Ladrio, you're not contractually bound, and this sort of thing has happened before, a teacher just ups and goes and Susan fills in until the next one arrives."

We cursed as we pulled our shredded stilettos from between the cobblestones of Via della Spiga, and I bought myself an unseasonably bright red wool dress with a deep scooped neckline and a tight waist and Megan bought me red shoes to match. She could not resist a sniff of approval when I tried them on and said they were definitely an improvement on the clogs.

Megan stayed with me that night to help me pack. The clothes she refused as gifts, alternating between "It's not really me Jools" and "Oh, but that's so you", I bundled into boxes to be collected the next day by a friend of Mrs C's who did charity work, the rest I forced into the one suitcase I had brought with me until it was past filling.

There were of course things so precious, so intimate, I could not abandon them to the hold, things which I packed into a small box while Megan was out collecting pizza and wine. On the bottom I put the three volumes of *La Divina Comedia*, a philosophy that was already acquiring significance in my life. In time I learnt that every love affair is a Divine Comedy of sorts. Like Dante's treatise on then contemporary beliefs, our amours are always a product of popular culture, but the starting point is culture itself – the romanticism of sex. The intended effect is indeed divine, the actual outcome is an eternal comedy of manners we enact every day, every night. Now I sit in the front row and smile, my ennui dispersing as the curtain rises, remembering how it felt, how it feels to be in love. I am always on the edge of going back.

And then there was the package that had arrived soon after my return from Florence. I retrieved it from under the bed, unwrapped the brown paper and ran my fingers over the smooth ivory calfskin of the cover, over the deep grooves of gold that formed the title. The book stirred memories of my own fantasy (or was it Mr C's?), and raised questions in my mind to which perhaps there could never be an honest response. Was the silken leash of my sexual temerity, the one that had pulled me back from that door in the wall along the canal, in any way comparable to the chains that bit into O's flesh? Had I been in need of annihilation? To free myself of a sexual conscience? Was I constrained by a learnt prudery or was I in possession of an intensely personalised need for autonomy, a sexual integrity that had everything to do with self control? I did know that unlike O, I had no need for pain; that was not my path.

Pain did not purify, pain was not the price to be paid for a pleasure beyond the constraints of the acceptable, pain was quite simply an indication that something was wrong. Pleasure was easy once the guilt had been understood and put in its place, which was invariably on the face of a dolorous martyr pierced through with phallic arrows. I have seen St Teresa in the throes of her ecstasy, it was mine every time a lover brought me to the moment of my orgasm in which the world was well lost.

But myself? No, I remained, renewed, remade. O and I, we would never agree.

I discarded the brown paper in favour of a gaudy silk scarf then placed the book on top of the others and layered all four with photographs and postcards of Italy. There was nothing of the American I could put in the box but the change of heart I carried within me. How I had changed I could not quite define. I know when I met him I thought I had very few lessons to learn, few experiences to garner that Italy had not already given me. He said he wished he could have been there at the beginning, to have met me at the airport that breezy day. He said that he wished to have been my mother, my father, to have grown with me from the child to the woman, to have been my first lover and my last. I smiled to myself; he had been and always would be sorely disappointed in that respect.

I filled the remaining space with lovely things lovingly wrapped in tissue and items of precious soft clothing and tied the box shut with yards of string – hand luggage, heart luggage – I would not let it out of my sight. The red dress I draped admiringly across the one empty chair.

Megan returned as the phone rang for the third time and I asked her to answer it. I was cutting up the pizza when she walked into the kitchen cradling the red wine to her chest and looking puzzled, "That was Jack. I told him we were having a girls' night in and that you'd call him tomorrow. How come he knew your number here? Is he pestering you or is there something you aren't telling me about you and Jack?"

"There's nothing about me and Jack, absolutely nothing."

"Good. Imagine his surprise when he finds you're gone!"

We neither of us slept that night but were remarkably bright to greet the day. Megan left me with hugs and tears in her eyes and a promise to write. I had many letters to write, to the children and a few of the kinder students. All those beautifully penned epistles! Such antique, such extravagant skills, not even needed now for a shopping list.

Mrs C had insisted on taking me to the airport and arrived in a beast of a car that roared into the square and growled with impatience as I gathered my things. Mrs C was surprised at the disparity between the boxes that were to remain and the one suitcase that was to accompany me – she knew how addicted I had become to shopping. I was travelling light, which was fitting, I had left so much of what I had been in Italy that my belongings were of little concern.

We did not speak on the way to Malpensa. From her taut face it seemed that Mrs C had many questions, but still she did not ask them. Having been so accepting of my sudden need to go perhaps she had started to question the reason? Perhaps puzzled, even disturbed at my departure, I was sure she was also relieved – to continue our affair when I knew more than she wanted me to would destroy the gentle balance of pleasured reciprocity. We had had our time together and there was nothing she could teach me now.

The ticket was waiting at the check in, paid for and first class, but her final gift was a Fendi purse lined with 100,000 lire notes, to spend on my next trip to Italy.

She kissed me at the gate. She kissed me on the mouth and slipped her tongue between my glossy lips; for once we were wearing the same red lipstick. My heart pounded and my breath grew fast as it always did when she kissed me, I would miss her beautiful tenderness. I wanted her to wrap her arms around me, to kiss my neck and push her soft breasts against mine, her cunt against my nakedness, but I pulled back and she stroked my cheek to wipe away a reluctant tear, "Do not cry *carissima*, you will ruin your make up."

I smiled at our mutual vanity and promised to write, then made my brisk way into the departure lounge. I did not look back but knew her eyes were on me. In fact many eyes were on me. I was wearing the red dress and the red shoes, not entirely appropriate apparel for a journey but just what I wanted to wear. As I moved through the smoky throng, my perfume mingling with the memory of Mrs C's, I was aware of the slip of nylon stockings on skin beneath my dress and of my nipples standing proud against the lace of my brassiere, and I did not seek to hide them.

I waited until the last possible moment at the gate, until the ground staff waved me through with their worried white-gloved hands and my hurried heels on the runway clicked through the hum of the engines, but when I reached the top of the steps and the stewardess' welcome one of them caught in a steel groove. I thought I was the last to board but as I bent down to remove my shoe and pull it free I realised that someone had mounted the steps behind me. I turned my head over my shoulder and saw the dark eyes of a young man staring into mine. I should have blushed, but I smiled.

The wool of my skirt was so fine that it had clung to my knickers so I had discarded them and wore nothing under the dress but the hold-up stockings Mrs C had given me. It was nothing that this man must have seen and nothing that had taken his breath away. He soon regained his manners however, and reached down to remove, with elegant fingers, my shoe from the rung. He held it before me and smiled a charming smile as he said, "*Permette Cenerentola*," and replaced the shoe on my foot, my scarlet toenails shamelessly visible through the fine nylon.

I thanked him, smoothed the dress down over my hips and walked past the astonished crew with all the aplomb of a catwalk queen as I wondered at the kindness of strangers and Prince Charming's seat number.

My Birthday

No more Prince Charmings for I am no princess nor yet a stately queen, no monarchist either but like the atheist I am who is awed by the creations of faith I do love the trappings of royalty. As I make my way across the lustrous tiles of my palatial bathroom to the throne before my dressing table I sense my skin tingling beneath the silk kimono. A reverberation of erotic memory? An old desire, revived by my recent proximity to the American? Surely not, and yet, and yet I am drawn to that small white rectangle propped against my perfume bottle and replicated in the mirror. He must have slipped it in to my jacket pocket. It looks so quaint, the typeface Garamond – I had not expected that; or the name above the many numbers –"Call me", it seems to say as I stroke its sharp edge.

My toilette becomes increasingly simple as I age. No more in possession of a porcelain-smooth skin I seem to have lost the need to cover it in a mask of powder and paint; a late-come vanity, I am told by women friends, due to the unnervingly persistent smoothness of my features and the acceptance of the few wrinkles I do have as the imprints of my smile.

I still have a passion for the pretty underthings I don with an air of seriousness which surprises me. My dress is simple and dark and my jewellery pearls, the short rope around my neck and the creamy spheres that drop from my earlobes. The shoes are not so high but arch my feet to a sufficient degree that I will need to walk a little slower than my usual rush – I have a tendency to shimmy even in bare feet.

I see my finger tremble as I press the numbers and when he answers on the second ring I know I blush. I can say no more than an absurd "It's me".

He sends a car, although as it glides through the traffic I think how lovely it would be to stroll through the park hand in hand like the young lovers we had never really been. I know the hotel, one of the more established bijoux residences close to where we met earlier. I am not surprised that he isn't there to greet me in the lobby – that would be awkward – I am not surprised at the pounding of my heart or the shortness of my breath as the lift slips up to the very top, to the penthouse suite, of course. I am not even surprised at the desire, nascent within me from the moment I heard his voice, and now fully formed and living in my blood. I am surprised however, at the surety, at the serenity of purpose I feel as I walk into his waiting embrace.